Wastoid

GITTE TAMAR

BTW LLC

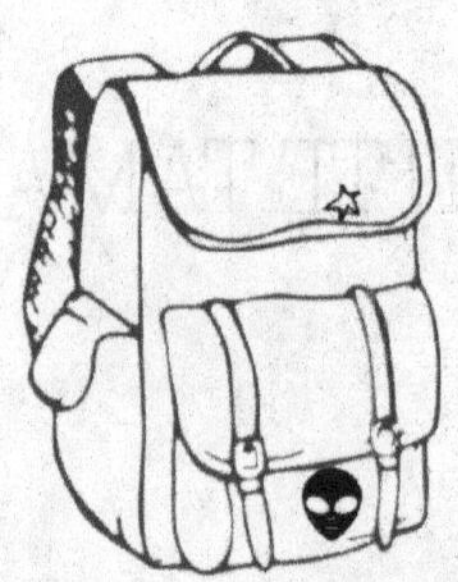

To those who struggle with overindulging in their vices, never feel ashamed for admitting you no longer want to be around each enticement.

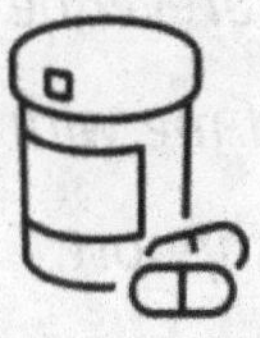

Acknowledgment

Thank you to each of my family and friends, you already know who you are, so I will refrain from listing each of your specific names. Just know I will forever be thankful for each one of you who provided me with never-ending troves of love and emotional support.

Thank you to all of my readers for continuing to embark on this journey with me. I am forever indebted to you.

WARNING:

This story includes references to death, abuse,
implied sexual situations/assault, some violence,
and, swear or curse words.

Contents

Chapter One

MY NAME IS ZOE

June 10, 2015, Somewhere in California

The desert extends for miles in the distance and mimics a backdrop from a Hollywood movie. Joshua trees and cactus scatter the dust-filled land while a gust of dancing wind sweeps across the sunny sky. As it lands on the dirt street, a dust devil forms on the ground, kicking sand into the air.

Without civilization in sight, the driver of a ratty 1990s Slug Bug convertible barrels down the road, bumping the music louder. A chipped coat of light-cream yellow clings to the metal exterior, which has a retracted top to match. Both headlights have glued-on curled black eyelashes to spruce up the car. With a black Sharpie, someone has doodled the name Tammy on the hood above one of the bulgy eyes. The cheap car stereo makes the grunge rock melody sound like it's coming from inside a tin box as it accompanies the sound of the pattering engine. On the back of the car, next to the steaming exhaust pipe, is a vanity plate. The letters spell out the name of the individual driving the vehicle, Zoe. Stuck to the dirt-smudged plate is an expired tag listing the last renewal year as 2014.

As the car hauls ass through the desert, the music on the radio becomes static as the young woman changes the station. Focused on turning the dial with her spastic fingers, she closes her eyes to make a wish and the car briefly swerves over the median of the two-way road. Landing on a station, Zoe listens to the first two words of the song and squeals with excitement. Her belting voice accompanies the familiar tune. The echo causes the wildlife to crawl back into their holes or take flight as the one-person party creates a commotion.

The only one in the car, Zoe looks to be seventeen years old. She exhibits restlessness and other stereotypical characteristics one would expect to see if they reenacted the role of a girl living on the edge in a movie portrayal. Her collar bones protrude from the base of her neck to her shoulders, connecting to her thin arms. As her bony hand clutches the car's wheel, it accentuates the muscle separation through her forearm, which leads to a slight bruise underneath the crease of her elbow and bulging veins running across her hands. Her thin frame dons a pair of torn light-wash jean shorts and a stained wife-beater that exposes her shoulder blades and looks like it was swiped from some man's closet.

Loving the sensation of her hair blowing in the wind, she presses her worn-out grass-stained Keds against the gas pedal, accelerating well beyond the speed limit. Her freely projecting laughter and fun-loving disposition leave no question that she likes to live on the edge. The scenery blurs as she speeds up, the transient wind revealing sporadic clumps of Kool-Aid coloring in her shaggy mullet. She shakes her head to rid the windblown pieces of dark brown and faded red that cling to the ombre-colored lenses. The transition of yellow and orange round plastic mimics the sunrise as it evolves through its morning routine.

Zoe's chipped black-polish-tipped fingers reach to adjust the rearview mirror. After quickly lowering it, she multitasks with her complacent dri-ving to check her appearance. As she lifts the sun-glasses to rest on top of her head to hold back her wild hair, her glazed-over eyes glance up at the dirty mirror's reflection, and she's spooked by what she sees. Her mascara and lipstick appear to be days old, and the charcoal-smudged eyeliner's overabundance contrasts with her blush-less face. Trying to fix herself, she licks the tip of her pointer finger and attempts to clean the smeared mascara under her eyes.

Giving up, she shifts her attention back to the blaring radio. Along with her disheveled appear-ance, she grows tired of the playing tune and searches for a different station to better express her mood. As her finger glides to the tuning knob, the car's tires hit a bump, causing her hand to flail and hit the keychain dangling from the igni-tion. The light sound of jingling keys makes her glance down. A green lanyard covered with pandas sways to the car's movement, and the visualization of them dancing while eating bamboo makes her smile. Attached to the silver keyring is a yellow fur-ry ball, color coordinated to the set of yellow fuzzy dice with black accents hanging from her rearview mirror. Hidden behind the keychain's pouf bobble is a simple metal pendant with a Narcotics Anonymous emblem.

Skipping past the charm's details, she rolls her eyes and continues her mission of changing the radio station. As her fingers graze the nob, her eyes shift up to check the road ahead while she simultaneously flips through the stations in search of new music. Anxiously she bites her lip, the harsh static between numbers on the dial makes her wince. Her ears notice a familiar female voice, and the alternation of upbeat songs and static abruptly stops. Immediately she cranks the music to drown out the car's struggling engine.

Punk rock grunge fills the air with lyrics about life's struggles of being shackled by the chains of past traumas.

As Zoe bangs her head to the beat, the bouncing movement makes her sunglasses fall to the bridge of her nose. The excitement of freedom makes her laugh, filling her with a sense of joy. "Fucking finally..." she says with a grin. Tapping the steering wheel, she pretends her long fingers are drumsticks as she beats a percussion-based solo. Her hands go wild as the song builds to the chorus, to which she sings along.

As the tune plays, the artist's relatability to her challenges and the warmth of the notes make Zoe believe someone else understands her daily struggles. Focusing on the road, she reaches for the stained yellow backpack on the passenger seat beside her. Patches depicting short phrases, miscellaneous aliens, and smiley faces—all affixed with rusted safety pins—encounter her fingers as she reaches for the zipper.

She unzips the front pocket to pull out a pack of Marlboro cigarettes, removes a single one, and shoves the box back into the canvas compartment. The burnt orange of her lipstick breaks up the color scheme of the white cylinder between her lips. She fumbles by her feet in search of a blue duct-taped barbecue lighter rolling around the driver's side floor. She grabs it and uses the top of her knees to steer the car while she lights the tip. Frantically she inhales a deep breath; a moment later, her face relaxes with relief as she blows out a cloud of smoke.

Upon making another attempt to fix her raccoon-like eye makeup, she glimpses the smudged mess through the lenses of her translucent glasses and throws them back on top of her head. Annoyed by her reflection, she elongates her reach and adjusts the rearview mirror toward her face. With intent focus, she balances the burning nicotine stick between the crease of her middle and pointer fingers and licks the tip of her index finger to erase the black smudges. Vigorously scrubbing her skin, she tugs it in different directions, like a candy maker pulling taffy.

As Zoe struggles to remove the charcoal-colored residue, her lack of progress causes the world to freeze around her and time to stand still. The purgatory thrusts her mind into a daydream, spiraling her into thoughts of past mistakes.

I know what you're thinking. How did a rock star like me get stuck in such a beater ride? This song brings me back to the good ol' times when things were easy... At least, that's how I remember it.

As she listens to the song loop back to the chorus, she can't contain her happiness about the memories she holds dear. Still working on cleaning up her eyeliner, she bangs her head to rid herself of the trials and turbulence of her life. She sticks her tongue out, admiring her new barbell piercing as she bounces in her seat to the song, and even though the skin around the jewelry is swollen and red, the sight makes her self-esteem flourish.

»»—•—••—•—««

My name is Zoe, and this is the story of my royally fucked-up life.

Chapter Two

DAMN THAT HURT

March 2015, Sketchy Tattoo Parlor

The radio playlist blares over the boombox, which is used as a makeshift sound system. Dressed in a fitted black spaghetti-strapped tank top with a ripped jean skirt, black fishnet tights, and black scuffed Doc Martens boots, Zoe sits on a red-vinyl-topped medical table. The semi-translucent sanitary sheet ruffles as she adjusts her posture. She eagerly sticks out her tongue, waiting for the shop owner to shove a blunt needle through it.

Her best friend, Britt, peers over his shoulder to see what's taking so long. About to turn seventeen, she's barely older than Zoe. She wears a pair of baggy vintage acid-washed jeans with a baby blue sweater she cropped to show her heart-shaped crystal belly button ring. Freshly curled locks of light-brown hair. She stands on the toes of her blue checkered sneakers to get a better view of her friend's monumental moment. The movement makes her thick locks sway across her lower back.

The tattoo artist's wobbling posture suggests he's under the influence of alcohol or narcotics. He attempts to regain his focus by running his purple latex-gloved hand through his box-lined beard. Even though his hair shows signs of gray, his rounded facial structure makes him appear around forty. A bleach-stained black short-sleeve shirt showcases his arm sleeves of faded second-rate tattoos, while his overstretched earlobes serve as frames for large silver gauges.

As he lines up the needle to the blue dot he placed as a marker on her tongue, Britt pulls her flip phone from her back pocket to document the wild night.

When the piercer shoves the needle through Zoe's flesh without warning, she winces. As the delayed stinging sensation sets in, a pool of water builds in her eyes, and she laughs with her tongue sticking out. "Is that all you got?" she barks.

Ignoring her comment, the artist concentrates on securing the flat back to the bottom of the piece of jewelry.

Britt rushes around him to get a close-up shot of the finished product, pointing her camera in Zoe's face as if interviewing her. "How does it feel, bitch? Let's look at that new bling," she says as she zooms in, squealing and giggling in high-pitched tones.

After finishing his placement, the tattoo artist slowly turns to the wannabe influencer and analyzes her immature behavior with skepticism. Something doesn't quite add up in his mind, and his gaze moves back and forth between the two girls. "You said you're both eighteen, right?"

Attempting to ignore him, Britt continues filming her friend, who sticks her tongue out, wiggling it at the camera.

Annoyed by their behavior, the man steps in front of her and points to two written warnings stuck to the wall with packing tape.

One states, NO FILMING ALLOWED; the other says, MINIMUM AGE: EIGHTEEN.

Zoe's eyes can barely stay open as an edible combined with a fireball shot kicks in.

Begrudgingly putting her phone away, Britt throws a tantrum by stomping her foot and grunting. "I already said yes to the age thing!" She reaches into a different pocket and pulls out a fake ID that has peeling plastic on the sides. "See? Seriously, don't have a cow."

He rips the identification from her long, freshly manicured robin's-egg-blue claws and closely analyzes the noticeable wear. His jaw clenches with irritation. Holding it closer to his squinting eyes, he tries to read the date of birth. "Never said I was," he states.

Recognizing he may not buy the validity of her ID, Britt works to maintain eye contact with the gritty-looking man while taking matters into her own hands. She flirtatiously takes the ID from his fingers and, taking a step toward him, reaches for the fly of his dirty dark-wash jeans.

Oblivious to the escalating situation, Zoe nonchalantly flicks her fresh addition out of her mouth until the mix of substances overcomes her, and she falls to her back on the table, laughing uncontrollably.

The flirtatious teen takes another step closer to the man. She bites her lip and softens her voice to exude a sultrier tone. "I'm sure you can let it slide, just this once. Wouldn't you like to join us in a little fun?" she asks.

The man's body stiffens from the abrasive advance, and he pushes the girl's hand away before she can touch him. "That'll be forty dollars. I can ring you up at the front."

Glimpsing past him, Britt winks at Zoe and shakes her hips as she turns her back. After a quick flirtatious glance over her shoulder, she pushes the back pockets of her jeans into him and smirks. While rubbing up against the guy to bide time, she peers at her friend and glimpses her bloodshot eyes. Britt scans the room until a red velvet curtain in the back of the store catches her attention. She lifts a finger and points to it. "How about we make a deal? I'll go with you to that private room for a pack of those grape Swisher Sweets behind the cash register and her piercing," she says, squeezing his leg.

Without a moment's thought, she grabs his hand and he follows her lead to the curtained-off area.

As they pass Zoe, he plants his feet and smiles at Britt's amused expression. "I tell you what... Depending on what's about to happen, I might be generous and throw in *two* packs of those grape Swishers," he says with a wink.

Capitalizing on his compliance, Britt leans closer to his ear. "Music to my ears," she states, tugging at his hand.

He points to her friend lying high on the table as he follows her. "What about her?"

Britt pauses and pretends to be naïve and confused. "Um...what about her?"

His eyes lustfully scan her developing curves. "Aren't you guys a package deal?" Zoe is oblivious, too high to understand what's happening, and solely focuses on feeling for the black tank top strap that's fallen off her shoulder.

Her bare skin makes the tattoo artist lick his lips with a craving intent. "I'll give you two packs of Swishers plus the piercing for free if she comes with." Tightening his grip around her hand, he leans closer to return a whisper. "I'll even let you keep the fake ID. It can be our little secret." The threat catches Britt off guard and her flirtation turns to anger. Muttering words of irritation under her breath, she stomps toward her friend and pulls her off the piercing table to join them. She glares at the man who's eagerly waiting. "Fine. We have a deal," she says.

His dark eyes spark excitement as his mind spirals into a perverted fantasy.

Too high to stand on her own, Zoe loses her balance, and her Jell-O-like legs collapse underneath her. Britt helps her to her feet and the two girls disappear behind the curtain.

Following close behind, the man shuts the velvet curtain behind them.

The ticking clock above the cash register, with its glow-in-the-dark hands, keeps track of their time behind the scarlet veil. Thirty minutes pass.

One by one, each of the three exits from behind the drapes. The man, first in line, angrily sprints ahead of the girls to the cash register. Britt apologetically chases him; upon catching up to him, she throws her hands in the air and loudly releases a frustrated sigh. "She said she was sorry!"

The man grabs a single pack of grape cigarillos from the cigarette wall. He glares at her as he slowly slides them across the glass countertop in her direction.

Britt rejects his attempt, sternly pushing them back toward him. "Come on. You said *two*," she says.

Once again, he pushes the package across the counter. A rustling sound breaks his glare, and his eyes shift to watch Zoe finally decide to emerge from behind the partition.

As she exits, her green face tells everything. Unable to walk in a straight line, she stumbles to the counter and sits on the floor with her head in her hands to stop the room from spinning.

Her severe inebriation makes the man angrily stew, and with his hand remaining on the pack, he signals to her slumped figure. "That was before I knew she was going to throw up," he states.

Before he can get another word in, Britt snatches the barter from the counter and rolls her eyes in disbelief. "She threw up on the back of the curtain...not you." Realizing her sass might hinder their ability to bargain for more, she catches herself and turns her furrowed brow into a seductive smolder. She lifts her eyebrows and adjusts her stance to push her hidden cleavage together. "She still performed, so don't be a jerk."

The tattoo artist slowly leans forward to match the level of her stare. "You still have a fake ID, don't you?"

Squinting, she shifts her smolder into a death glare to intimidate him.

Her attempt doesn't faze him and the immense effort makes him bust out laughing.

Immediately her face turns red with frustration, and she snaps. She flips him off and yells, "Fuck you!" as she walks toward the door. Once she's at the exit, she realizes she has left her friend on the floor, so she turns around to get her. "Come on, Zoe. We gotta bounce."

Seeing a shadow standing over her, Zoe lifts her head to look and laughs at her friend uncontrollably. "Bounce..." she repeats.

With a clenched jaw, Britt yanks her companion to her feet.

"Jesus!" Zoe says as she rubs her arm. As she dramatically takes a pause, her face makes a delayed wince. "Who pissed in your Cheerios?" she asks. Unable to keep track of her surroundings, she doesn't realize her friend has moved behind her.

Trying to get Zoe to move faster, Britt pushes her back with both palms, directing her to the exit.

After reaching the door, Zoe plants her feet and turns around. She sticks out her tongue and flips off the tattoo artist with both hands.

Britt's mouth drops open, and she laughs. "I've got to get on your level because this shit is whacked."

As the girls stumble out of the shop giggling, the man plasters on a disingenuous smile and lifts his hand in a sarcastic wave.

The shop door jingles with their exit, and the door closes.

Wiping the fake smirk from his face, he rush-es to the door and locks it behind the girls. He expresses his anger, aggressively flipping the sign from open to closed.

The signage hitting the glass makes them jump, and Britt rolls her eyes as they move away from the entrance. "Geez," she grumbles.

Zoe clutches her cheeks in pain without a sec-ond thought about what happened inside the tattoo parlor. "Ow, ow, ow," she yelps. Her irritation builds with the cold, damp air outside; to distract herself, she holds out her hand. "I need your phone."

Britt stares at her like she's just heard a joke and robustly laughs. "Why?" she asks.

"I want to see what the fuck this thing looks like," Zoe says, grabbing for the air. Becoming impatient, she tries to assess the damage and goes cross-eyed. With her tongue sticking out, she panics. "Is it swollen?"

Tired of listening to her complaints, Britt pulls her phone out and passes it to her. "Love ya, bitch," she states with a kissy face.

With her new piercing showcased, Zoe flashes a goofy smile and grabs the phone. "You think Adam would still like me if my face permanently looked like this?" she asks. Not waiting for a response, she opens the phone to observe her reflection in the back-facing camera.

Her updated appearance distracts her, and she dramatically nods to get Britt's attention. Loving her new look, she analyzes every inch of her piercing on the small screen and the view inspires her to pose for some photos.

The only thing on Britt's mind is the social media posts she might miss by letting her friend use her phone. Trying to distract herself, she takes a tube of bubble gum pink lip gloss from her front jeans pocket and applies it. "Ugh, Zoe. It's so annoying that your dad confiscated your cell. Seriously, he treats you like a baby. It's ridiculous."

Enjoying the commiseration, Zoe pauses from taking a selfie to roll her eyes in agreement. "Tell me about it," she says. The camera clicks as she snaps a picture while pointing to her tongue. "After he sees this, I'll probably never get it back."

Worried her friend may pocket her phone, Britt laughs nervously and snatches her lifeline back.

Zoe's response to the missing phone is delayed, and her finger clicks on the nonexistent device to take another photo. As soon as she realizes what happened, she glares at Britt. "Hey!" she exclaims. Miffed, she throws her hands on her hips.

"Phone privileges are only for positive people," Britt says. Waiting a moment, she notices Zoe's face is irritated, so she tries to make a joke. "You look hot!"

Zoe's frown washes from her face and she cracks a smile.

Observing her shifting personality, Britt realizes her ploy is working and plays off the positive vibe. Quickly she turns the phone's camera back on and leans toward Zoe to take a selfie together. "Say NDY!"

The unfamiliar acronym confuses the rebellious teen, and she contemplates as the camera sounds with a click to capture the moment. "What's NDY?" she asks.

Ignoring her, Britt checks the photo and becomes irritated. She repositions the camera to get a better angle for their selfie. "I love how you're such an alien sometimes," she says with a fake laugh. As she tries to hold an open-mouthed smile to pose for the picture, she notices her friend waiting for a better answer. "It means 'not dead yet'… It's like you but way better."

Zoe loves the response, and her eyes widen as she sticks out her tongue for the photo. "NDY!" she says.

Before anything else can trash the image, Britt snaps a pic and the camera resonates with a high-pitched click. "Yasss, queen!" she squeals. As she flips through her options to find their photo to post, she sees her friend frantically rubbing her cheek.

Zoe winces and gives a dramatic sigh. "Why does my tongue hurt so bad?"

Thinking she's ridiculous, Britt stops what she's doing to laugh at her misery. "Dude, it just got stabbed with an ice pick, and then you gave that guy a blow job..."

Zoe stands dazed as her memories flood back to her like a tidal wave hitting a beach. Britt shoves her shoulder to snap her back to the present. Her high wearing off, she shakes her head and laughs to make herself feel better. "Yup, now I remember. Yikes."

They both burst out laughing at the situation and share a moment of solidarity. Zoe's body shifting back from her high makes her head ache, and with a look of defeat, she places her head in her hands. Without hesitation, Britt ceases her laughter and rummages through her pockets.

After finding what she's searching for, she pulls a small repurposed mint box from her baggy pants. "I know something that'll help," she says, shaking the bottle beside her nauseous friend's ear.

The familiar noise makes Zoe's illness vanish, and she perks up like a kid at a candy shop. Sticking out her tongue yet again, she pretends she's taking communion and smiles as the pill hits her taste buds. Without a drop of water to wash it down, she swallows.

Satisfied with helping her, Britt pulls a dime bag of weed from her bra and rolls a blunt. She pulls a scratched-up hot-pink lighter out of her pocket, lights the blunt, and takes a hit. Her eyes droop, and she coughs as she blows out a cloud of smoke. "This shit is fire," she says, admiring the burning bud. Swiftly she shoves the weed into her friend's face. "Come on—take a quick hit before we catch the next Metro."

Zoe grabs the joint from her hand and takes a long inhalation before loudly hacking to catch her breath. "Shit, it's strong. Where did you get this?" she says, passing it back.

Britt grabs it, takes another drag, and smirks. "You remember Dale, right?"

The name catches Zoe off guard, and she takes a step back and gives her friend a skeptical eye. "You mean Big Dick Dale?"

As Britt considers the remark, she nods and giggles. "The only decent thing he ever gave me. I take that back—the *second* decent thing he ever gave me," she states as she holds the weed in the air. With her other hand, she reaches into her back pocket and pulls out a tin case to save the half-smoked joint for later.

They both chuckle and look toward a bus stop across the street.

Zeroing in on the realtor photo advertisement printed on the back of the bench, Britt checks the time on her phone. Her eyes become panicked. "Oh, shit, we gotta hurry. The bus will be here in five." She grabs her friend's hand and lunges toward the busy road.

Together they run across the street while dodging scattered oncoming cars. As they reach the faintly lit bench, they notice the dim streetlamp overhead highlights a Sharpie-drawn mustache on the realtor's face. Both try to hold in their laughter, scanning the scattered group of seedy characters waiting for the bus.

Eyeing the street for the bus, Zoe spots a pair of headlights approaching. Her nervous energy kicks in, making her legs antsy. As she fidgets, she clutches her tightly crossed arms. "What if he hates it?"

"Hates what?" Britt asks as she scrolls through social media on her phone. After finding what she was searching for, she proudly holds up her screen to show her best friend. Moving it closer, she points to the number of likes they've received on the selfie she posted of them together outside the tattoo parlor. "OMG, you've gotta see this! Adam was the first to like it, and you know what that means... He's pretty much in love with you."

The words intrigue Zoe and she moves closer to look.

Noticing the bus doors opening, Britt rips the phone away from her face and shoves it back into her pocket. "Stressing out over it will only make your forehead wrinkle," she says. She grabs her friend's hand, lifts it to her lips to give a quick kiss, and pulls her to follow.

They race ahead of everyone to be the first ones to get on.

Trying to act sober, Zoe refrains from peering down and stumbles. Her reflexes don't kick in, and she face-plants on the floor of the bus's dirty aisle.

Britt turns around to look. "Bitch, you are an absolute mess," she says with a laugh.

The driver pushes back her graying hair, exposing her glaring timeworn eyes and irritated expression over their drunken behavior.

Zoe slowly wobbles to a standing position and brushes herself off, oblivious to the bus schedule or the passengers trying to find a seat. Britt turns to the driver to defuse the situation. "I'm so sorry about my friend," she says, then takes a small step closer and shifts her loud tone into a whisper. "It's her time of the month, and the doctor prescribed her something for cramps. Obvs, he screwed up and gave her way too high of a dose. The guy should be sued or something."

The fifty-something woman has had enough of their shenanigans and points to the back of the bus with her thumb.

Sensing the animosity, Zoe straightens her posture to appear sober.

Annoyed that they're wasting her time, the driver raises her voice to get them to move. "No one cares about your business. Just hurry and sit down. You're holding up the line," she says.

Trying to orient herself, she turns to face the disgruntled crowd waiting to get on the bus and lifts her hands. "Sorry—" Zoe says with a slur.

Britt turns, scanning the angry faces with an apologetic expression while snatching Zoe's arm to stop the rest of her speech. Dragging her along, they laugh as they make their way to the back of the bus.

Everyone follows behind to find their seats quickly as the bus pulls away from the stop.

An older man with a cut-off shirt and long gray hair sitting across from them turns to stare, cracking his lips in a cynical grin, revealing a mouthful of missing and nicotine-stained teeth.

Britt's mouth pops open with disgust. "Ew, as if!" Her comment doesn't deter him, and his behavior escalates as he makes provocative gestures at the two girls.

Zoe turns to him and sticks her finger toward the back of her throat to make a gagging face. "What the fuck?" she says.

Britt anxiously taps her shoulder as the bus screeches to a stop in Oakwood. "Perfect timing. It's our stop. Let's go!" she says, standing up.

Not budging, Zoe stares at the creepy man across the aisle. As they glare at each other, she scrunches her face to avoid blinking.

The man's excited body language makes it obvious he enjoys the game. Contorting his face in reply, he opens his smile wider, allowing enough space to poke his wiggling tongue between his decaying teeth.

Upon realizing she hears no following footsteps, Britt stops and pivots to look behind her. Seeing the seedy exchange, she immediately runs back to retrieve her friend. Annoyed, she frantically waves her hands in front of the duo's locked focus. Still not getting Zoe's attention, she leans close, huffing sighs of frustration and snapping her fingers while shouting her name.

The sounds assault Zoe's ears and the puffs of irritated air entering her glazed eyes make her blink.

Enjoying his win, he chuckles at her dismay.

Zoe throws her hands into the air. "Fuck," she snaps, then turns her head to glare at her friend's angry face. "You made me lose the staring contest." No longer able to maintain her stern demeanor, Britt smirks at her friend's ridiculous reaction.

Zoe rolls her eyes, having no patience for the sarcasm over her loss.

The bus groans as the doors slowly close.

Both girls hear the noise and realize they're losing time making their escape. Their eyes widen.

Britt quickly turns toward the front of the bus and yells at the top of her lungs. "Wait! This is our stop!"

The driver recognizes the shrill voice from earlier. Irritated, she refrains from turning around and stares into the rearview mirror to assess the situation. "Oh, Lord, here we go," she says, shaking her head as Britt and Zoe stumble down the aisle toward her.

As they make their way to the front, they brace themselves by grabbing onto each stained seat top and metal pole they pass. The door's hydraulics release a giant squealing huff of air as they open; Zoe covers her eyes to avoid eye contact with the angry driver's penetrating glare as she passes her. "Thank you!" she shouts, sprinting out the door and down the stairs.

Frustrated, the driver purses her lips and shakes her head in disbelief. "I tell you, some people just shouldn't be parents." With an irked pull of the handle, she shuts the door, almost catching the girls' mid-exit.

The bus's fuel-guzzling engine revs as it barrels off into the distance.

Chapter Three

SHWASTED

March 2015, The Streets

The street is empty. Multiple streetlights are burnt out, and the few that have remained lit aren't bright enough to provide adequate lighting. Boarded-up brick buildings surround Zoe and Britt, plastered with graffiti and hand-drawn fliers advertising concerts, strip bars, and parties. It's a rough part of town. Random piles of trash riddled with takeout containers and squished cups from fast-food restaurants scatter the grunge-stained sidewalk. A full moon reflects bits of warm yellow lighting onto the urban scenery, illuminating a murky mud puddle near the girls' feet.

Zoe reflects on the bus driver's last comment, which fills her with mixed emotions. Offended and unable to let it go, she opens her mouth in disbelief. She then spins around to face Britt. "That's just rude. She def would be the worst parent ever!"

Ignoring her concern, her friend continues to walk ahead.

Zoe turns around, taking a moment to scan the scenery. The glistening puddle sparks her attention and her feet skip forward to admire her new piercing in the water's reflection. The muddy hue makes her smirk with an idea, and in a single fluid motion, she drags the scuffed toe of her beat-up Doc Martens boot through the contaminated liquid, rippling the still water. With a flick of her ankle, she kicks the street's murky mix at the prissy teen's back.

Sensing cold droplets on her skin, she scans the sky for rain clouds. Hearing her friend's chuckle, she checks the back of her pants and notices spots of brown on her jeans. "Gross!"

Zoe laughs like a hyena, which makes her stomach cramp.

Britt's face turns a pissed-off shade of red. She darts toward the culprit behind the stains on her pants and attempts to kick water at her with all her might.

Zoe dodges the attempt, and as she turns to rub her victory in her friend's face, she trips on a large crack in the sidewalk. As she falls to the dingy ground, her ungraceful landing creates a nasty rip in the fishnet lacing of her tights.

Loving her friend's dismay over the twist of fate, she laughs. "Karma is a real bitch." Quickly, she takes her phone out of her pocket to snap a picture. "Stay down there so I can get a pic."

"Like this?" Zoe asks as she dramatically crawls on the sidewalk. Continuing to feed off the moment's energy, she looks up and makes a seductive face for the camera.

Britt tries to contain her hysterics as she stumbles forward to get a better angle. "Work it, queen!" Her intoxication worsens by the minute, and she becomes a photographer for an impromptu model shoot. She leaves her friend in the middle of a pose sprawled out on the ground to check the series of photos. "Dude, you gotta see this pic... You have a massive rip in your tights."

The tear has become more significant because of her crawling movements, and her eyes widen with disappointment. She throws her hands into the air.

"Why does shit like this always happen to me?" she says, lying defeated on the ground with her hands covering her face.

Britt comes to the rescue, prancing toward her disheartened friend lying hopelessly sprawled across the filthy concrete. Reaching into her jeans pocket, she pulls out her trusty mint box. Not wasting a minute, she opens it and offers Zoe a small white pill. "Take this. You need it more than me; that bruise will be wicked sore tomorrow."

Zoe peels her fingers from her eyes to survey the recommendation. Noticing the thin rectangular shape and slight linear markings, she immediately realizes it's Xanax. Like a flip of a switch, her eyes light up, and her attitude shifts. She snatches the pill. As she pops it into her mouth, she smiles and crawls like a stripper toward Britt. "Why are you so great? I couldn't have a better friend."

Reveling in her performance, Britt smirks at her relaxing state. She shrugs, then leans over to help her up. As she struggles to lift her intoxicated friend, she grunts to emphasize the difficulty. "Um, obvi... Because we're besties for life."

Zoe nods in agreement as she sways side to side and fumbles to her feet.

Britt shifts her focus and checks her phone for the hundredth time. "Shit! Oh, my God, girl, it's way later than I thought! We gotta get it together; we are so late." As if synchronized with her realization, her phone lights up. She glances at the screen and gasps. "Dale texted me! He's at a party!" Her fingers move at lightning speed as they type a response.

Thinking her friend's ridiculous behavior over a guy is comical, she attempts to wink, but can't. Her intoxicated state causes her eyes to lower and her chin to fall to her sternum. The new visual perspective leads her to glance at the large hole in her tights, and she panics over her disheveled appearance. "Wait. Do you think Adam's there?"

Britt's eyes remain locked on her screen, and though listening, she finishes her text before responding. Upon hitting the "send" button, she places her hand on her friend's shoulder to stabilize herself, setting the tone for a serious heart-to-heart. Zoe's growing state of intoxication causes her ability to process speech to slow, making Britt's words seem disjointed. "Zoe, listen to me," Britt says. "We're going to Adam Schaffer's house... That's where the party is, so yes, he'll be there."

The answer wasn't what she wanted to hear. Filled with angst over the confirmation, she stares blankly toward the end of the empty street to avoid making direct eye contact.

Britt shakes Zoe's shoulders to rein her attention back toward her. "Snap out of it! The guy is in love with you." Looking at her pupils dead center, she drives her point home. "You'll be fine."

Nodding, Zoe releases a sigh of relief, knowing the words are accurate. Her mouth cracks a slight smirk. "Okay, I guess you're right," she says, rolling her eyes.

The lighthearted smile on her friend's face is contagious. Feeling a sense of accomplishment, Britt grins back and releases Zoe's shoulders. At ease, she lets her arms freely swing by her sides as she walks down the street.

Zoe follows and forgetting about her torn tights, happily twirls.

Hearing giggling and the echo of tapping feet behind her, Britt turns, walking backward to face her friend. Entertained by the girl's impulsive behavior of interpretive dance steps, she laughs. "Ho, I have a question, but you've gotta be honest with me."

"Go ahead. Shoot," Zoe answers, her hands waving in the air.

"How many benzos did you take before we met up today?"

Spinning like a windmill, Zoe almost runs into Britt while trying to count.

"Our tolerance is the same, and you're selfishly so much further gone than me," Britt says, using her hands to stop her friend's momentum.

Trying to steady her feet, Zoe stops her dance moves and uses her fingers to help count. It becomes a game for her. Jokingly, she holds up several variations of numbers. With each combination of digits she puts up appearing blurrier than the last, she moves them closer to her eyes to focus. As her hand multiplies into three, she chuckles. She holds up the fingers of her right hand and shoves them into Britt's face. "This many..."

Britt silently squints at Zoe's fingers, and her mouth drops open in shock. Impressed by her friend's party mentality, she seizes the position of her flat palm to give her a high five.

As her hand swings to connect, Zoe tries to meet her halfway but misses.

Britt watches Zoe's momentum uncontrollably follow the path of her arm. She grabs her by the shirt, barely stopping her tumble forward before she hits the ground. "Shit, bitch. You're raging tonight."

Zoe laughs, and breaking free from Britt's grasp, does a happy dance. In a state of euphoric bliss, she stumbles ahead, skipping with her heavy feet. Her pace quickens, her lumbering hop steps turning into a gallop. "Catch me if you can, loser!"

Britt watches her friend move farther down the street. "If it's going to be one of those nights, I'll need some more magic pills." Reaching into her jeans, she pulls out the bottle and takes another. She shakes the bottle and listens to the rattling sound, estimating how many pills are left. Pleased by her stash, she places the bottle back in her pocket for safekeeping and prepares for a wild ride. *We need to get to the party before those set in*, she thinks. *We can't have a repeat of the last time.* She watches her friend's silhouette move farther in the distance and chases her down the street. "Wait!" she calls out.

Giggling at Britt's urgent tone, Zoe dramatically stops to wait for her.

Out of breath from her sprint, Britt huffs as she swings her hand and jokingly tries to hit her friend's arm. Even though Zoe dodges the punch, she still reacts and winces as though she's in pain.

"So dramatic." Britt's eyes squint as she tries to keep them open. "You remember what happened last time our night started like this?"

A chilly breeze drops the air's temperature, causing them to pick up their walking pace.

"You mean at the house party with the bonfire?" Zoe replies.

"Yeah, when we climbed into the back of that red pickup and fell asleep watching the stars."

The vivid memory from the prior week makes Zoe cackle. "Dude, thank God that guy only lived down the street from my old man's house or we would have been screwed. Who knows where we would have ended up?" The thought sends a shiver down Zoe's spine, and she shakes her head to stop it.

"Better question: who doesn't check the back of their truck before driving off?" Britt says.

Shrugging, Zoe gets an idea and mischievously smiles. "I'd be down for a repeat. That night was hella fun," she says.

"True. Just no naps in trucks this time," Britt replies.

The longer they walk, the more intertwined their steps become. Seeing a distant streetlight marking the end of the block, they look at each other and sprint. They laugh as they make it to the end. As music blares with a loud bass from an approaching crossroad, the girls turn to identify its location.

Britt grabs Zoe's hand and pulls her staggering friend toward the residential street, which is packed with rows of parked cars. "We gotta hurry before all the good booze is gone." They walk for what seems like a century to the girls' tired feet. Britt checks the time on her cell phone and is surprised to see only ten minutes have passed since the last time she checked.

Cars line the suburban neighborhood street that leads to the home where the music is blaring: a white two-story house with navy-blue trim. Solo cups cover the unmaintained front yard. College kids drunkenly stumble over red plastic intermixed with calf-high weeds as they disperse onto the street, turning the party into a block-long event.

They've found the party. As Britt and Zoe head toward the chaos, they admire the incredible turnout. While passing through the neighborhood, they survey the cars tightly parallel parked. Both girls scan to see which ones they recognize to give them a heads-up on who they'll encounter at the house.

Britt spots a familiar beat-up Honda with chipped paint and gives her friend's hand a few squeezes. Pointing to the discovery, she squeals with excitement.

Zoe's head turns at a snail's pace, and she scrunches her brow to focus. "What?"

"Eek. Don't you see Dale's car! That means he's here!" Tugging Zoe's hand, she takes a big step forward. "Come on. Let's find him!"

Something seems off, and not having a good feeling in her gut, Zoe tries to express herself. "You sure you want to—"

Britt, not wanting anything to spoil her desires, cuts her off. "I said come on," she says, giving Zoe's hand another jerk.

"Fine." Yielding to her friend's persistence, she moves forward.

Their substance-fueled pace picks up to a stumbling run to the car.

Britt notices the back park lights are on, releases Zoe's hand, and walks up to the hazy driver's-side window. Frantically she taps the glass. "Dale," she says.

The interaction doesn't surprise Zoe. This is typical of Britt and Dale's dysfunctional relationship; in fact, she's witnessed it many times. Observing her knocking and his lack of response, she takes a step back to give her friend space.

Britt's face turns red with anger and her finger taps harder. "Dale! The lights are on, so I know you're in there. Open the door before I break this F-ing window!"

Still keeping her distance from the unfolding scene, Zoe stands stock still, her eyes glazing over.

Britt retracts her hand in preparation to pound harder. Suddenly the window rolls down, exposing a small gap. Smoke pours through the slit and into her face. She dramatically coughs and fans her hand in front of her. "Jesus, you trying to hotbox the outside too?"

The window descends a bit farther, revealing a twenty-year-old college student holding a joint and wearing a junior college football team letterman's jacket. Even though Dale barely made the team as a walk-on, his cocky demeanor matches that of a signed NFL player. His pink-stained irises are scarcely visible in the smoke-filled interior as he peers through the partially open window. "Whoa! What's shaking, little mama?"

Irritated that she can't fully see inside the dark car, Britt frantically tugs on the handle of the locked door. "Let me in." Realizing she probably appears crazy, she masks her intensity with a giggle. "I'm not mad—I just want a hit of what you're smoking."

Dale flips the automatic door locks off and on to mess with her.

The game makes Britt angry, and she loudly and impatiently grunts.

Dale is having the time of his life making a game of her frustration until he's struck by a memory from a prior volatile encounter. His demeanor shifts and he says something calming, worried if he pushes her too far, she might wreak havoc on his car. "Whoa, don't kill the mood, little mama."

The tactic momentarily lessens Britt's fury until the sound of a jean zipper echoes from inside the vehicle.

Britt's eyes grow wide with disbelief and her imagination runs wild. Suspicion fills her head as Dale turns away from her and directs his attention toward the passenger seat.

A girl in her early twenties with overfilled lips and blond extensions adjusts the brand-new implants protruding from her bustier. When she lifts her head from Dale's lap to see what's causing the commotion, he immediately pushes it back down and smirks. "Wasn't talking to you, babe. Trust me; everything's just fine."

Britt stands staring at the car in shock. She leans closer to peer through the limited opening as she tries to get a better look at the girl. "Who the fuck is that?!" Unable to keep her composure, she kicks the car door in a fit of rage. "Bitch, I will beat your ass if you don't get out of the car. I mean it!"

Hearing the threat, the girl stops what she's doing and sits up in her seat. Staring across the driver's side seat at her harasser, she uses the back of her hand to wipe her mouth and smirks, then casually pulls her half-chewed piece of gum from the dashboard and pops it back into her mouth.

Dale places his arm around the blonde to pull her closer and ease the animosity of the situation. She gazes at the man cuddling her and loudly smacking her gum, blows an enormous bubble.

He playfully pokes it with his finger and pops it. Smiling, he scans side to side at each of the young women. "Baby girl one, meet baby girl 2.0."

Proud of her new title, the blonde straightens her posture and pushes her boobs together. Lifting her hand, she waves by wiggling her fingers. "My name is Trix," she says.

As she finishes her introduction, Dale lightly kisses the back of her hand and passes her his lit joint. Seeing she's content, he redirects his attention to the window.

Lost for words, Britt glares in silence. Zoe, no longer able to contain herself over the ridiculous situation, laughs hysterically. The uproar breaks the silence, rattling Britt's nerves. "Don't be a fucking asshole, Zoe!" she squeals. "Stay out of this!"

Dale rolls down the window another inch to look at Zoe and lifts his chin to acknowledge her. "Hey, home girl. What's popping?"

Through a fit of laughter, Zoe salutes him and yells back a sarcastic remark. "Glad to see nothing's changed."

Britt turns around and punches her arm to shut her up.

Glaring back at her, Zoe rubs her aching arm to numb the sting. "What?"

Ignoring her, Britt turns back to the car and yells through the window's opening.

Staring at the back of her head, Zoe mocks her by making mimicking faces while tuning out the sound of her friend's shrill complaints.

❈ ❈ ❈

Thinking back to the memories of her interactions with them, she drifts off as her mind combs through each of her experiences, remembering that *this usually goes on for a while. It's typical of their relationship and not the first time Dale has cheated on her. Honestly, I'm not sure why she always goes back to him—probably for the free weed. The first infidelity was with a sorority girl who proudly wore a lousy ombre dye job. That was the only detail regarding her appearance that Britt told me about. It was right after they got into a relationship, and Britt was visiting him for the first time at his college dorm. She drove to campus one Saturday afternoon to surprise him. With an excited smile and one quick knock, she flung the door open, only to find him in bed with her. Britt was livid. What do you think he did?*

He threw up his hands to claim surrender and said, "It's not what it looks like."

After that, she stupidly forgave him, and I stood by her side.

The three of us went to a house party a few weeks later, and no surprise, Dale disappeared. Britt and

I searched everywhere for him and, in the process, saw some shit we didn't want to see—his car was parked outside the house with the taillights on and the inside dome lights off. Rather than reading between the lines, Britt approached the vehicle. Dale didn't care; he was in the backseat making out with some platinum-blond twenty-year-old he'd met at the party. She was wearing a tight dress hiked up to her waist. Britt was oblivious. Keeping her attention on her social media notifications, she opened the passenger door to get inside. She even apologized to him.

"Sorry I took so long, babe," she said. "The bathroom line was hella long."

When she finally glanced up from her phone, she noticed he wasn't in the driver's seat and turned around to check the back.

"What the fuck?!" she exclaimed.

What do you think Dale did when she caught him? He put his hands up, and just like the time before, he said, "It's not what it looks like."

Again Britt forgave him. Things seemed good for the next few weeks until we were all riding around in Dale's car and stopped at a gas station so he could pick up some weed from a guy who worked there. He left us in the car with instructions not to go anywhere but didn't consider that we had pounded a few shots just before the drive, so Britt had to pee. She held it for as long as she could. Anxiously looking out the window to see what was taking so long, she felt she could no longer hold it and would wet herself.

"If I make it quick, it should be fine," she said.

Not asking my opinion, she sprinted out of the car, and I followed to make sure she was okay. The next few minutes were like something out of a movie. She grabbed the knob and shook it vigorously, only to find it locked. In desperation, she pounded on the door.

"Someone's in there!" the cashier yelled.

Stopping her neurotic knocking, Britt crossed her legs while she waited. Lo-and-behold, the knob turned and the door opened. Dale emerged with a nineteen-year-old girl with tanned skin, an A-line bob, and a leather miniskirt. Met with his shocked girlfriend's face, he paused and eyeballed her as she peed herself.

Guess what he did next? He held up his hands as if under arrest and said. "It's not what it looks like."

I hoped the third time was the charm, but as I've learned, love can be blinding.

Fast forward to that backyard party when we fell asleep in the back of a red pickup. We hitched a ride there with some random guy she had picked out to make Dale jealous. As we pulled up to the get-together, Dale was out in the open with a beer in his hand, sitting on the back of his car's open trunk with a half-clad stripper in her mid-twenties sitting on his lap.

Ignoring the guy who gave us a ride, she rolled down the car window and shouted obscenities. Not feeling she was getting Dale's full attention, she jumped out of the vehicle as it rolled to a stop and continued her rant.

"We're done!" she screamed.

In typical Dale fashion, he threw his hands up in the air and said, "It's not what it looks like."

My honest opinion is that our night escalated because she tried to numb her dramatic disappointment. That breakup lasted for two days, tops.

A few days ago, the last instance occurred at this same house. Dale doesn't have a lot of ambition. In fact, by choice, he doesn't have his own place and tends to couch-surf for housing. That home's sofa was one he crashed on frequently. Reiterating his loser *nature is beside the point; by now, we'll all know that he's a scrub.*

The party started off as expected. By the end of the night, Britt and I were pretty lit, and needing a smoke, we stumbled to the patio. While lighting up, we heard weird moans coming from the bushes to the left of the home's back entrance. It freaked us out, and we were sure it was a ghost. Britt investigated the noise, and there was Dale with some twenty-year-old female wearing a two-piece metallic clubbing outfit. Shocker... Well, it shouldn't have been, but Britt still seemed surprised.

"Dale!" she said, clenching her fists.

I still remember her slack-jawed expression as she angrily pulled her fresh cigarette from her lips and threw it onto the concrete. She was so mad that she didn't even bother to finish her smoke before storming off. Gotta hand it to him—the guy is consistent. Upon being caught, Dale looked at me and threw his hands in the air.

"You got to understand it's not what it looks like."

All I could do was shrug. I knew it was exactly what it looked like.

⇉ ·•·•· ⇇

The sound of yelling and aggressive tire kicking snaps Zoe out of her daydream. She mutters to herself still thinking of the many other times Dale has been unfaithful. "Told you so."

As Dale peers out the cracked window to watch his manic girlfriend trash his tire, he notices Zoe stumble sideways. Cracking a smirk, he realizes she's high. "Always good to see you in your prime," he barks.

Thinking the sarcastic comment is in reference to her angry outburst, Britt rushes to his window to yell at him.

Chapter Four

MR. NICE GUY

As Britt yells at Dale through the cracked window, sounds of screaming and laughter from the house party tamp down her escalating verbal abuse.

Lifting her hand, she thinks for a moment about getting Zoe's attention, then lowers it to her side. A loud group drinking beer in a circle on the distant lawn distracts Zoe, and she turns her head to look.

Dale sticks his hand through the opening of the driver's window and points at her. "Ask Zoe. She knows you're crazy."

Hearing her name referenced causes her head to snap back to her friends, and they immediately pull her into the conversation. Her feet tap on the ground with nerves as her right-hand lifts to signal Dale to cut her out of the argument.

"She's my fucking friend, not yours! You can't ask her stupid questions like that." She attempts to grab Dale's pointing finger through the window but misses.

Feeling threatened, he raises his voice.

Trix casually interjects her opinion, and the un-invited spontaneity causes the other two to grow louder.

Worried they may try to pull her back into the argument, Zoe maintains eye contact as she slowly takes a giant sidestep away from the disagreement and toward the party. After executing the move-ment, she stays still like a stone statue, quietly waiting to see if anyone has noticed her disen-gagement. Insults and screams assault those in the Honda.

Zoe shrugs at the fact that no one cares about her lack of participation in their tiff. Relieved that her slow departure has gone unnoticed, she re-leases an enormous sigh. Turning her body to-ward the party's joyous and raucous noise, she heads toward the yard. Paranoid Britt and Dale might figure out she's gone, she tries to remain quiet by lengthening her steps like an astronaut walking on the moon. The smell of filled plastic cups makes her smirk as she finally reaches the house's glorious lawn. As she makes her way to the action, she encounters a frat star passed out on the edge of the overgrown grass with what appeared to be a hand with its middle finger extended, flipping everyone off, drawn in Sharpie on his forehead. The early-college-aged boy wears a pair of camel-colored Sperry loafers and tight pastel shorts that hit above his knees. His polo shirt is a baby blue with a light brown stain on the front, and his messy sun-kissed hair wildly strays in every direction. One wrist sports an oversize scratched silver-toned Rolex stolen from his father. A pair of tweaked Oakley reflective sunglasses with over-sprung hinges lies beside him.

His wasted appearance makes Zoe feel better about herself, and she chuckles at his disheveled state. Her curious eyes shift to the pair of stray sunglasses. Her legs feel like they're floating on clouds as she moves toward them. Squatting, she reaches to pick them up and pauses as something else catches her attention.

A red Solo cup with a yellow sticky note attached to the front sits perfectly upright next to the guy's sprawled hand.

Enticed, Zoe grabs it and, without delay, reads the note aloud under her breath. "Drink this when you wake up." The message makes her chuckle, and she sniffs the liquid contents. Unprepared for the stench, she jolts the heavily liquored drink away from her face. She then looks from side to side to see if anyone is watching. Without a care in the world, she shrugs and chugs the liquid. Drinking the concoction too fast causes her to release a loud burp. She crushes the cup between her palms and then throws the trash next to him as she stands up and redirects her stumbling steps to the home's entrance.

Everything is a blur as her fingers touch the doorknob and her surroundings slowly spin in a psychedelic orbit. The sticky handle turns underneath her lethargic palm as she opens the door. Filled with euphoria, she stands in the entryway. As a group of frat brothers exits past her, she shimmies around them to enter.

Inside, strobe lights highlight every ounce of the house's trashed state. Even the wooden beams in the archway above Zoe's head have suffered chips and deep scratches. The entry opens to the living room with two matching stained beige checked cloth couches and a folding card table set up in the middle as a makeshift coffee table.

As Zoe's feet take a few more steps, they stick to the beer-soaked wooden floor, and she temporarily pauses. The intensity of the lighting variations overstimulates her half-functioning mind. The strobes add to her nausea. She shields her eyes with her hands and flees straight toward the kitchen, sure that if she doesn't get out of there, she'll embarrass herself in front of her crush by upchucking all over his floor.

The intoxicated college kids scattered throughout the room pay no attention to her behavior. They're used to seeing weirder shit and, frankly, are too wasted to notice by the time of her late arrival.

Hurrying past the dining area, Zoe quickly finds herself in the kitchen, and upon entering its stable fluorescent lighting, she lowers her hands from eye level. Trying to reorient herself, she staggers into a row of cherry oak cabinets and braces herself on the chipped marble island in the center of the room. To sober up, she focuses her wavering vision on the countertop's marble pattern, and immediately her stomach calms. Taking a therapeutic breath, she lifts her head to see if she recognizes any of the party's boisterous voices.

The dining room opens into the kitchen, the standalone island's the only divider between the two. A dwindled group of diehard partygoers circles an old, dark wood dining room table. On the tabletop, in the center of the festivities, are several small baggies of snow-white cocaine, some of which has been poured out and divided into lines.

Knowing she's found the fun makes her smile, and she takes a moment to watch each of them take their turn with the straw. Her eyes light up as the last person in the group steps forward to get his fix.

It's the infamous Adam Schaffer. His spiked frosted-tip hair matches the color of the font on his letterman's jacket, and the addition of a football-shaped patch labels him as a football jock.

Finishing his line, he raises his eyes from the table. He makes eye contact with Zoe, giving her a smoldering smirk.

Her cheeks blush as she gives herself a mental pep talk: *It's only a few steps; you got this*. She takes a deep breath and smiles at her crush, pushing her incoherent self off the counter, then stumbles toward him.

"Look who decided to show up," he says.

His words make her bashful. "I..." She tries to respond, but the butterflies in her stomach override her speech. Adam is the only person in her life who puts her at a loss for words, and the feeling is foreign to her. As she holds her breath to focus on appearing sober, she stands a few places down from him at the table. Tightening her posture, she tries not to sway.

As Adam moves around the table to stand beside her, Zoe stares straight ahead at the wall to avoid making eye contact with him.

Believing she's playing hard to get, he lightly chuckles. "I thought you'd never show."

His voice sends nervous shivers down her spine, making her smirk. She shifts her head to look him in the eyes and coordinates a response. "Oh, yeah?" Worried she sounded stupid, she pinches her leg to punish herself.

Enjoying his control over her, Adam leans in closer to whisper in her ear. "Don't tell anyone, but I only put this party on so I could see you."

The validation of his affection toward her makes her even more smitten. She diverts her eyes and seductively bites her lip.

Disregarding the clear signs that she's infatuated, Adam continues to act as though he needs to win Zoe's attention by setting up a line of cocaine as an enticement.

She admires his doting nature and, having never experienced a functional relationship, she views his act as a validation of his deep care for her; the simple gesture triggers her to fall harder for him. She gazes into his eyes as he finishes cutting the line into place. "You sure know how to make a girl feel welcome," she says.

Adam's pearly white smile puts a substance-laden hex on her.

Acting quickly, Zoe releases her grip on the table, grabs the straw, and snorts up her allocation of the powder. She grins as her nostrils sniff the air, then stumbles back from the table.

Adam catches her wobbling frame, keeping her upright. Gazing into her eyes, he wipes the residual white powder from the bottom of her nostrils. His lips smirk at her intoxicated state. "You look good tonight—like really, really, good."

The compliment makes her blush, and her chin drops as she tries to glance away.

Adam places his hand under her jaw, stopping her head from descending farther. Noticing her eyes drifting closed, he playfully nibbles her earlobe to keep her awake.

His tactic works, and she giggles.

"Maybe we should do a repeat of last weekend," he says, leaning in even closer and whispering. "You know how you turn me on when you get freaky." Embracing her in a hug, he wraps his hand around her thigh and squeezes her leg.

Zoe is helpless.

Only wanting one thing from her, he takes her hand.

The room is spinning; Zoe stabilizes herself with his grip and smiles as she follows him away from the table.

Watching her stumbling feet, he shakes his head and gives a playful chuckle. "Zoe, Zoe, Zoe, whatever will I do with you?"

With her limited ability to focus, Zoe doesn't fully process what he's saying and merely giggles in response. As they exit the kitchen and head into the living room, the strobe lights overwhelm her escalating state of intoxication. With all the power she can muster, she tries not to trip over her feet.

Noticing her slowing pace and her grip tightening on his hand, he twists his body to check on her. He can tell her consciousness is waning and knows he must hurry. Disregarding her well-being, Adam doesn't allow a moment of rest and pulls harder to get her to move faster. He smirks as he maneuvers her around the couches in the staircase's direction. He then takes a deep breath and hoists Zoe up the first step to get her momentum going.

Unable to keep her focus, she trips partway up the staircase and falls forward across several stairs. He releases his grip on her hand and stops to peer down at her slumped body lying on the steps. Acting as though her intoxication is cute, he chuckles to himself and pretends her demeanor is flirtatious and not sloppy. "Oh, are we playing this game again?"

As she focuses on not throwing up, she rests her head against the stained green carpet runner that clings to the edge of the step.

Worried she might be on the verge of passing out, Adam playfully bends over, picks her up, and throws her body weight over her shoulder like a firefighter rescuing a damsel in distress.

She flails her limbs as if to put up a fight, and her wiggling makes her nausea worse. "Put me down. I feel sick," she says. Trying to avoid vomiting, she temporarily submits to Adam's dominance and hangs complacently over his body like a lifeless ragdoll.

He masks his irritation with a passive grin. As his face turns red with anger, he transforms her plea into a joke and disregards her words. "That didn't stop us last time," he says.

"I mean it this time," Zoe says, then covers her mouth with her hands.

Rolling his eyes, Adam ignores her and continues to carry her up the staircase.

Flailing her limbs, she begs him to put her down.

As they reach the top step, his annoyance becomes apparent, and he can no longer hide his temper. Her coiled fist hits the spine of his back, and he snaps. "You're making a fucking scene!" he barks. Wanting to inflict pain, he pinches her thigh.

The residual sting makes her wince, and she gives up.

Her cooperating deadweight makes him happy. "That a girl!" he says as he slaps her ass. He slowly sets her down on her feet, then grabs her jaw to focus her attention. He isn't the same doting individual from the kitchen, and his pointed gaze spurs feelings of resentment. "Don't you ever try that shit again—you hear me?" Leaning closer, he whispers through his clenched teeth, "Next time I won't be so forgiving."

With the threat diminishing her self-esteem, Zoe smirks and bites her bottom lip to lighten the mood. Her eyes droop closed to mere slits as she playfully unzips Adam's jeans.

Enjoying where this public moment is heading, he aggressively places his hand on her head to guide her to the floor to go down on him. He bites his lip to quiet himself, and as she finishes, he zips up his pants and wraps his fingers through her hair to help her stand.

The gesture makes her feel dispensable, and her embarrassment feeds into the nausea building in the pit of her stomach. Unable to stand on her own, she reaches for the wall to provide a crutch for her tingling legs and avoids making eye contact by peering at the floor.

Zoe's sheepish nature makes Adam feel powerful, and he stands taller, reveling in his dominance. "You get your tongue pierced?" A pleasure-filled shiver rolls through his shoulders as he relives the spontaneity and a cocky smile forms on his lips.

Zoe moves her hand up the textured white wall to better balance herself and nods "yes."

Adam shrugs at her struggle. "It's hot," he tells her.

The pain from the jostling of her new piercing has a delayed onset, and she grabs her head with both hands to make it stop. Zoe loses her grip on the wall and stumbles to the ground. Unable to keep her eyes open, she blindly sticks out her tongue to show him where the pain is coming from and points to her barbell piercing. She switches her voice to the sound of a seductive, pouting baby, hoping to garner pity from him. "I need a Xannie; my tongue hurts," she whimpers.

Adam immediately reaches into the back pocket of his jeans and pulls out a small baggy of various pharmaceuticals. Each of the marked pills varies in shape and color.

The sound of the shaking makes Zoe smile from ear to ear. As Adam waves it closer to her face, the rattling entices her eyes to crack open. As her hands dart forward to collect the reward, he pulls it just out of her reach. "Not so fast," he says slyly.

The sight of her empty hands makes her pout.

Taking his time, Adam tauntingly opens the small bag made from translucent plastic and waits until her desperation has peeked before presenting an ultimatum. "Let's make a deal," he says. Leaving her in suspense, he slowly digs through the baggie to sort the pills. Finally locating what he's searching for, he pulls out a tablet. Pinching the drug between two fingers, he holds it in front of her. "I'll give you one of these."

Seeing his blurry digits move closer gives her hope, and she acts like a cat batting at a toy filled with catnip.

Adam jerks his hands away from her grasp. "You can have one under one condition: you'll owe me a fuck," he says with a smirk.

Considering they've had numerous sexual encounters, she sees the solicitation as no big deal and rolls her eyes. Her fingers form into a pulsating fist as she holds out her hand for the pill.

The frivolous, uncaring nature of her relinquishing her body makes Adam's chase seem effortless, leaving him disappointed. The catch was too easy, driving him to seek another element to escalate his adrenaline. He prefers a struggle or frisky fight to turn on his covertly sadistic mind.

Adam's hot-and-cold demeanor irritates her. Hungry for the drug, Zoe quickly retracts her twitching hand to get to the bottom of his sadness. "What the fuck now?" she asks.

Mirroring her on a roller-coaster ride of emotions, he turns his frown around and flirtatiously sticks out his tongue.

Zoe grins. Following along, her mouth gapes open, and she sticks out hers as far as it will go. The overextension of the appendage strains her face, and her eyes squint shut. Sitting quietly, her tongue extended, she waits until she detects the chalky texture of the pill on her tastebuds. Closing her mouth, she trustingly swallows it as though it's a church communion wafer. The sensation of the dry medication traveling down her throat fills her with a tinge of euphoric peace, and her lips crack a smile. "Mmmm."

He intently watches her. The feeling associated with causing her sensory experiences to flourish inundates his mind and body with a sense of ownership. While she basks in the effects of the drug traveling through each vein, Adam moves his body closer. Placing the remaining bag of pills in his back pocket, he grabs hold of her chin to guide her head toward his, then delicately kisses her forehead.

The imprint of his wet lips on her skin makes her giggle. Opening her eyes, she gazes at him with a yearning for someone to care and once again naively believes his minor gesture confirms the unconditional love she seeks. A wave of butterflies complements the escalating high, and her giggles become uncontrollable. "I'm so fucking numb right now I can't feel my face," she slurs. The rolling laughter causes her to fall to her back. Lying on the floor, she clutches her cramping stomach while trying to catch her breath.

Rather than being concerned about her wrecked state, Adam, turned on by her vulnerability, leans over and slaps her ass. "Well...aren't you funny?" He scans her body with his thirsty pupils and imagines tearing the clothes off her thin frame. "I'll be back. Just gotta do something real quick. We'll pick up where we left off in a minute."

In a world of heightened intoxication, Zoe continues to giggle and rolls to her stomach. Her body mimics the movements of a roaring tiger as she tries to look cute and convince him to stay.

Halfway down the stairs, he stops and turns back to face her. "You remember where my bedroom is, right?"

Still positioned on all fours in her animalistic pose, Zoe nods and smiles.

Smiling back, Adam winks. "Good. Now take your perky ass there and wait for me."

He completes his descent down the steps and disappears into the crowd of incoherent partyers. Scanning the space for familiarity, Zoe struggles to locate anything recognizable to help orient her to her surroundings. Her jelly-filled limbs press against the nearby wall, using it for stability. Unaware of her body's signals, she doesn't compute how high she truly is. She labors to rise to her feet but falls to her knees as the world around her spins in an unprovoked orbit. The intoxication she's experiencing differs from her usual Xanax trips.

Something isn't right.

During a fleeting moment of clarity, she recounts the image of the bag of shaking pills, and her mind races.

»—•—«

What did he give me? Desperately she tries to shake the thought of his potential deception. *He cares,* she thinks. *He loves me.*

Taking a deep breath, she locks eyes on his bedroom door, which is located at the end of the hallway.

Unlike the others lining the hall, the door is painted dark blue, making it stand out from the rest.

Using her upper body to support her, she crawls toward it. After several minutes, she completes the trek, coming face-to-face with the targeted entrance. The sight of the doorknob triggers thoughts of exhaustion. Unable to stand to grasp the handle, Zoe gives up, shimmies to the wall next to the door, and props her back against it. Thinking a moment of calm might help tame her downward spiral, she rests her head in her hands. The action doesn't aid in refocusing her vision, and her surroundings become so blurred that they're unrecognizable. Her eyes roll as she fights to keep her unnaturally heavy lids open.

The sound of approaching footsteps grows louder. Zoe desperately covers her ears to dampen the muddy shrill tormenting her ringing eardrums, but her hands are useless. A pair of dirty sneakers sit in front of her slumped body. Everything feels disjointed, almost like an out-of-body experience. The ringing dissipates, taking her hearing with it. As she uses her frozen pupils to slowly scan the shoes, she notices Adam's loafers nearby. His presence puts her mind at ease and comforts her as she nods off.

Her blatantly intoxicated state excites him, and he nudges the guy standing next to him.

As a twenty-year-old kid taps his foot nervously, his spiked chocolate brown hair remains glued into position. His clothing choice of a pastel pink polo and accented shoes to match leaves no question that he's a frat boy. His hazel eyes display a look of skepticism as he scans from side to side.

Adam pats the guy's back, signaling him to move closer to Zoe. "See? What did I tell you? She's good to go."

Still unsure, the guy glances at her, then back at the boy who facilitated her unconscious state.

Feeling the transaction is taking too long, Adam fidgets. Trying to speed things up, he holds out his hand for payment. "Come on, dude. She took enough downers to tranquilize a horse. Even a

D-1 lineman wouldn't remember a thing after that dose." He extends his hand farther while scanning the hall to make sure no one is around. "So pay up."

Helplessly watching the exchange play out, Zoe tries to open her mouth to speak, but nothing comes out: her muscles are paralyzed.

The frat brother fumbles for a wad of mixed cash in his pants pocket, then anxiously slaps it in the middle of Adam's palm.

He quickly counts the money to make sure he hasn't been ripped off. "Cool. Seems to be the full two hundred." He shoves the cash into his front pocket and motions his head toward her. "She's all yours."

Gathering a tiny spurt of control over her fingers' motor function, Zoe slowly reaches her hand toward her crush's shoe to elicit help.

Ignoring her silenced plea, he bends over, picks her up, throws her body over his shoulder like a sack of livestock feed, then reaches for the handle to his bedroom door.

The john follows close behind, his hands sheepishly wedged into his pockets.

As he twists the knob, he pauses and turns back to utter a disclaimer. "The only rule I have is that you can't damage the goods." Lightly chuckling, he smirks. "I'm planning on using them later."

The frat guy smirks back and gives a head nod to show his understanding. He then motions for Adam to wait outside. Swiftly he opens the door and, without hesitation, carries her to the unmade bed and carelessly tosses her onto it.

Everything in the room wreaks of stale weed and body odor.

Adam bends over Zoe's limp body to whisper assurances into her ear. "Don't worry; it'll be over before you know it, and then I'll buy you something nice." As soon as he delivers his message, he springs to his feet to avoid any potential response and shouts to the frat guy, "Your hour starts now!"

Jittery with excitement, the guy races into the room. As they pass each other, Adam casually pats his shoulder and exits before slamming the door behind him.

The college student smiles to reveal the slightly off-kilter placement of his teeth. Even though they seem straight at first glance, a closer inspection reveals a few overlapping each other; it perfectly accents his covert narcissism.

Everything is a blur to Zoe, and her numbed body makes each sexual advance manifest as if it's a false reality. The only memories of the horror are her buried feelings of disgrace and the taste of sweaty beer on the guy's warm breath. To counteract the terrifying violence, she closes her eyes to pretend she's somewhere else, then passes out.

Chapter Five

BROKEN DREAMS

Disregarding the horror transpiring in his room, Adam grabs another drink from the kitchen and mingles with the guests. He passes back through the living room and spots a tan sorority girl with chestnut-colored hair. As her fringed crop top sways to the beat of the music, he makes eye contact with her and seductively smiles. Trying to decipher how much time he has, he quickly glances at the top of the stairs and listens.

The distant mattress creaks and headboard thuds complement the beat of the house music.

Knowing he has time to kill, Adam redirects his attention to the mystery girl dancing across the room and walks her way. As he passes, he pretends to bump into her unintentionally. The force of their collision knocks her off balance. "Oh, I'm so sorry!" he says, helping her to her feet. "I'm Adam."

"I know who you are, Mr. Quarterback. I've seen you play before," she says with a bashful smile. "I'm Madison."

"With those looks, you sure your name's not Angel? Because your perfection could only have come from heaven."

Madison giggles.

They flirt back and forth for a moment, and then he passes her his phone. "I feel like there's a deep connection here," he says.

Smiling, she scans the screen. Quickly she types in her number and reaches out to hand it back to him. "Call me."

Infatuated by her beauty, Adam smiles in return. Taking his phone back, he peers at her saved number and notices the time.

⇥⸱⸱⸱⸱⇤

Two hours have passed.

"Fuck," he mutters.

Madison appears concerned.

Realizing he spoke out loud, he covers his panic with flirtation. "Time flies when I'm with you."

The compliment makes her blush, and her smile grows wider.

Out of the corner of his eye, Adam recognizes the frat guy fleeing down the stairs while zipping his fly. He covers his anger by feeding off Madison's smitten demeanor and locks his gaze more intensely with hers. Taking her hands, he makes her feel special. "Unfortunately there's something I've got to tend to, but I promise this won't be the last time we see each other."

She seductively bites her lip as her doe eyes watch him leave.

Not looking back, Adam sprints up the stairs. His heartbeat increases as he enters the hallway and notices the frat guy left the bedroom door open. Worried his erratic behavior will raise suspicion, he regains his composure and slows his pace to a brisk walk down the hall. He then enters the room and quietly shuts the door behind him. "Honey, I'm home," he says sarcastically. Peering across the room, he sees Zoe is still unconscious and vulnerably sprawled across the mattress.

As he approaches her, he realizes her eyes are closed, and she's unresponsive.

Trying to remain silent, he removes his shoes, gently places them on the floor, and tiptoes to the bed. Softening his demeanor, he sits down beside her. He admires her peacefulness and leans over, kissing her forehead. While caressing her hair, he stares at her. "You know I love you, Z."

Zoe doesn't respond or move a muscle and remains passed out from the heavy sedation. Adam tucks her under the covers to make her more comfortable. After removing his shirt, he pulls out half a sleeping pill from the baggy in his pocket and swallows it. Before the medication can set in, he strips down to his gray boxer briefs, climbs on top of Zoe, and kisses her neck.

He falls asleep beside her just as the sun is rising.

⋙—••—⋘

Each ray of tinted orange light accents the plethora of empty red Solo cups scattered across the lawn. Remnants of the wild night have been generously strewn inside and out. Even the large pine tree in the front yard fell victim, littered with multiple rolls of streaming two-ply toilet paper.

Compared to the previous night, the street appears abandoned, with Dale's blue Honda the only vehicle left in sight. The car's passenger door slowly squeaks open, exposing its lack of maintenance. The commotion wakes a flock of bluebirds in a nearby tree, all of which chirp happily.

As Trix exits, she shields her eyes from the sun while grasping a detached clump of stringy bleached-blond hair extensions. Yawning, she appears confused by the previous night's love-triangle altercation and wonders how the handful of hair escaped her head. The sound of the tiny bird's joyous song torments her sensitive ears. She slams the door shut behind her, hoping to silence them, but her attempt fails. Unwilling to give up on a mission to stop them, she targets the birds' location, removes her heels, and charges the tree they call home.

The chirps grow louder as the creatures fly away in unison.

With nothing else to take her anger out on, she turns back to yell at the idle blue car. Lifting her middle finger, she flips off the remaining passengers. "Your dick isn't good enough for me to be dealing with this shit." Her irritation builds from the lack of response. Proudly lifting her head, she storms off down the street, strutting as though her walk of shame is taking place on a New York City catwalk.

The car's tinted windows fog as she struts away, and the singing birds land back on their branched perch. Still upset by the altercation, they emit panicked squawks, sounding like nature's alarm.

Lying on top of Dale, Britt is the first to hear the noise. As she wakes up, she attempts to dispel the fresh headache from the front of her head with a yawn. "Oh, God," she says. "What time is it?" She reaches out to clean a section of the fogged glass to peer outside.

Her jostling movement wakes Dale from his snoring slumber. "I don't know, baby," he replies. Shifting his demeanor, he smirks, "Fuck o'clock?" He laughs.

Ignoring him, Britt squints a single eye open to peer out at the brightness outside. The surrounding scenery confuses her, she turns her body and peers around the car's interior to collect clues. Scanning each item, she attempts to jog her memory regarding what transpired the night before and discovers a single extension left on the passenger's seat. The ratty hair, at least twice as long as hers and the opposite color, immediately sparks the memory of Trix.

Hearing her breath grow heavy with anger, Dale glances at the passenger seat to see what's upsetting her. The sight of the stray hair makes his pupils widen. Thinking quickly, he tries to defuse the situation by playing naïve and pulling Britt's body in tightly for a suffocating cuddle. "Everything okay, babe?"

Britt pushes herself away from his bare, cheaply tattooed chest and smacks her clenched fist against his sternum. "Why don't you ask your girl, Trix?"

He peers around with a look of confusion, pretending to be dumbfounded by the name. "Who?" His hands wrap around her waist. "Come on—you must have had a bad dream. Let's cuddle."

Disgusted by Dale's pattern of lying, she slaps his hands away and her body fills with anger. "Don't act like you don't remember the skank from last night!"

Realizing words alone won't cover his escalating lie, Dale smiles with a smolder to draw Britt in as he tries again to pull her closer to his chest. "Baby, baby, baby," he coos. Grabbing her hand, he lightly caresses the back of it with his lips. As he slowly looks up into her eyes, he grins. "You know I only got eyes for you."

Britt intensely surveys his body language to read his intentions and, giving up, focuses deeply on his gaze.

Annoyed by the time she takes to give in to his whim, Dale dramatically rolls his eyes. "Come on," he urges her. Inching her closer to his chest, he uses his manipulative charm to draw her in. Slowly turning his head to scan the empty seats, he continues with his speech. "She ain't even here." Seeing her posture relax, he smiles to drive his point home and win her back. "The only fine woman I see is the one in front of me." He then flirtatiously taps her nose with his index finger and softens his voice to talk to her as though she's a child. "Do you know why that is?"

Infatuated by his words, Britt bashfully glances down at his chest and tries to cower to act innocent. "Why?"

The return of her pushover nature excites him; to reward her, he grabs her by the ass and delicately kisses the tip of her nose. "Simple, because you're the only woman for me."

With a smirk, Britt kisses his neck. "Is that so?"

The tickling sensation makes Dale smile and nod.

Wanting to please him, she continues to make a trail of kisses from his neck to his chest. A sliver of bright light escapes through the small clean smudge on the window and shines into the car's interior, making her stop abruptly.

Bothered by the pause, Dale frantically tries to get her to keep going. "What's wrong? Why are you stopping?"

Glancing out the window, Britt rubs her eyes. "Geez, what time is it? It's so bright out."

Dale tries to redirect her attention by grabbing her face and kissing her. "I don't know." His lips smirk with careless flirtation. "Lovin' time?"

Immediately she pulls away and sits up. "Oh, my God, Dale. Stop it. I'm serious." After brushing her self off, she hoists herself over the backseat and onto the center console, flicking the extension to the floor. She acts disgusted while slumping into the seat once inhabited by Trix.

"I mean it! It's like super-fucking bright out. My dad's going to kill me!"

Realizing how stressed she is, Dale gives up on his flirtation. He exits the car, climbs into the driver's seat, and shakes the set of keys dangling from the ignition.

Britt bites her nails, her eyes darting to the steering wheel.

Quickly Dale starts the car. The engine revs. "Come on, girl. I'll drive you home."

Slowly she lowers her fingers from her mouth and stares at her savior. Her eyes light up. "You're the best, babe!" Springing toward him, she kisses his cheek and sits back down to buckle up.

"You know I always got my girl," Dale says, pulling away from the curb.

Britt rummages through her pockets in search of her tube of baby pink lip gloss. Upon finding it, she pulls down the car's visor, exposing a mirror. Admiring her reflection, she applies it.

Annoyed by her lack of attention toward him, Dale removes his right hand from the steering wheel, taps his cheek, and tilts his head toward her. "Don't you owe me a li'l something?"

His words break her fixation with her reflection, and after putting the mirror up slowly, she rolls her eyes in response. Releasing a large breath as if tasked with emptying the dishwasher, she leans toward him and kisses his cheek.

After wiping the glossy imprint from his skin, he smirks over his win and places his hand back on the steering wheel.

Britt pulls her phone from her pocket to sift through her social media feed as she repositions herself in her seat. A new post causes her pupils to become dilated with excitement. "Eek!" She zooms in on the photo to get a closer view and dramatically gasps. "No way! I knew he was, like, so in love with her."

Her excitement makes him curious and pulls his attention away from the road. "What are you talking—"

Before he can finish his sentence, she shoves the phone in front of his face for him to see the picture.

"Jesus, babe. I'm driving." The car slightly swerves as he tries to catch a glimpse. "I can't afford to get another ticket. My insurance is already through the roof." His actions contradict his scolding words, and he shifts his gaze to quickly scan the photo. "Whoa, wait, is that Adam Schaffer?" He acts surprised. "I didn't know he and Zoe were a thing."

Britt retracts the phone and holds it closer to herself to analyze every detail.

The picture shows Adam and Zoe standing at the dining-room table at the party. He has his hand flirtatiously around her waist. Zoe's eyes are barely open, and her tongue, fully extended, is licking his cheek.

An idea pops into her head, and she squeals. "Oh, my God! I could do matchmaking for a living... Ugh, I am so good." She zooms in on the picture to better investigate the surrounding details.

Her screech causes his face to wince, and he rubs his right ear to stop the ringing. "You can't be making that noise while I'm driving."

Britt ignores him, her attention solely fixated on the photo. "I mean, look at their chemistry... His arm around her tells me he's obsessed, and she's the happiest I've ever seen her."

As she continues to read their body language, Dale gets increasingly irritated.

"OMG, she's even licking his face." She zooms in on his handsy grab, examining precisely what he's grasping and the tightness of his grip.

Dale's eyes dart to see if she is still obsessing, then return to the road. He fidgets in his seat. "Yeah, cool. Just tell Zoe to be careful. I've heard some things about that guy."

The notion of oncoming gossip makes Britt's ears perk up. Her attention shifts from her screen toward him. "Like what?" she asks, glaring with impatience. He clenches his jaw and gulps regretfully over saying anything that might have compromised bro code. "You know, guy stuff..."

She repeats her question louder. "Like what?"

Her assertive demeanor makes him nervous. He speaks faster, the pitch of his voice elevating. "All I'm saying is Zoe is a cool girl, and I don't want to see her in a bad situation." Dale refocuses on the road to avoid eye contact. "He's older, you know? He's been around the block."

His cryptic words don't communicate the omen he had hoped for, and she punches his arm. "Baby, you're older than me, so what's the big deal?"

Wincing, Dale fills with a sense of relief. Even though Britt didn't take his message as a warning, he believes he did his part to help and smirks to lighten the mood. He playfully shrugs and winks. "True, but I'm one of the cool ones."

She smirks back. "I know." Diverting her eyes, she looks out the window and quickly spouts, "That's why I love you."

Her profession of feelings surprises him, and his nerves flutter. With crimson cheeks and tense posture, he stutters a response. "You l-love me?"

Thoroughly enjoying making him uncomfortable, Britt smiles at his avoidance. "Do you love *me*?" She gives him her undivided attention and grabs his crotch.

Dale takes a large gulp of air as he fumbles for a response. "Um, um, um... I mean..." His nervousness runs wild, triggering his eyes to dart haphazardly at the surrounding scenery. "There are many things a man loves in life..." Spotting a basketball court in the distance, he points his trembling finger at it without thinking. "Like basketball!"

His response leaves her dumbfounded. "Like basketball? You're seriously comparing my love to a recreational sport?" She sits farther back in her seat and crosses her arms. "Dale, that's a *hobby*."

Knowing he messed up, he stares straight ahead and grips the steering wheel tighter. After a moment of silence, he lets his left hand steer and reaches across to fetch something from the glovebox.

Britt glares at his rummaging hand and continues to pout.

Dale pulls out a joint from an emergency stash in the compartment and places it between his lips, then frees his hand to grab the lighter from the cup holder. Lighting it, he inhales.

Seeing the open glove compartment annoys her, and she uses her knee to slam it shut.

The harsh sound causes him to inhale smoke down the wrong pipe, which makes him gasp and cough. Trying to catch his breath, he rolls down the window. "I think I just need some air."

Noticing Dale's face turn red from choking on the smoke, Britt uncrosses her arms. Her concern for his well-being washes away her anger. "Seriously, are you okay?"

As he clears his throat, he nods and passes her the joint.

The free weed makes Britt forget the irritating conversation. After taking a hit, she blows out a cloud of smoke and, still thinking of the social media post, smiles. "Adam fucking Schaffer. I can't believe they're a thing." She peers out the window in a daydream state. "I'm sure they went at it like animals last night." Resting the joint between her lips, she pulls out her phone to view the picture again.

Dale's edginess subsides in sync with the whites of his eyes turning pink, and he chuckles.

Taking another hit off the joint, Britt blows a ring of smoke into the air and happily laughs. "What a lucky bitch. I wonder what they're doing now. We need to plan a double date pronto."

⋙ ⋅⋅⋅ ⋘

As the two lovebirds continue with their morning drive, the same bright rays of sunshine that prompted Britt's anxiety about returning home late reveal the eerie reality of what transpired at Adam's house. Even though the kitchen photo she'd been admiring received many likes, it no longer reflects the reality of the current scene.

Without the lively rally of the partygoers, the celebratory energy is no longer present. The morning light exposes the trashed home, voiding all romanticized memories from the night before. A light dusting of cocaine and a sticky paste-like substance created from spilled beer cover the dining-room table. New stains of unknown origin add disgusting character to the couches. The card table, once used as a makeshift coffee table, now lays flat, its legs splayed in four different directions. A single overflowing black garbage bag sits in the middle of the living-room floor. Excess cups, bottles, and beer cans, unable to fit in the confines of the plastic, are scattered from the home's interior to the street, identifying without a doubt the origin of the previous night's chaos. Everything is quiet, the muted chirps of birds outside replacing the sound of blaring house music.

Upstairs, in Adam's bedroom, Zoe is disoriented as she slowly opens her eyes. At first, she doesn't know where she is. Lifting the sheet draped over her, she sees her naked body. Instantly she drops the tan percale fabric to cover herself out of embarrassment. Concerned about what she might see, she reluctantly tilts her head to look beside her. Adam is snoring next to her, passed out and sprawled facedown. The familiarity of his stark-naked body gives Zoe a sense of relief because regardless of what happened, at least she didn't hook up with a stranger. As she gathers her bearings, a shooting pain emanates from inside her mouth, and her hand races to clutch her cheek. "Ow!" As the word leaves her mouth, she realizes she shouted and glances at Adam to make sure she didn't wake him.

With a monstrous snore, his body slightly shifts to get more comfortable.

She sticks out her tongue and focuses on identifying the cause of the immense pain. The touch of her finger against the barbell triggers the recollection of when she got the piercing. Remorseful of her decisions, she mutters, "What the actual fuck?" As she internally berates herself for her mistakes, she slowly turns her head to look back at Adam and forces a smirk. "I guess at least I did something right." Her head throbs and guilt-ridden anxiety overcomes her. Each of her thoughts ridicules her choices. *Why would someone like Adam ever want a mess like me? God, I wouldn't even want me.*

The sound of him yawning causes her to freeze. His eyes remain closed as his head turns and his body rustles.

Adam scoots closer to cuddle and slowly opens his eyes to look at her. "Hey there, beautiful," he says with a grin and a gravelly morning voice. It's difficult for Zoe to contain her worry. Did she embarrass herself last night? The uncertainty of her actions consumes her, and she attempts to change her demeanor by forcing a smile on her face.

Adam chuckles. "You were wild last night."

Unable to mask her anxiety, Zoe pulls away to hide her body. "Wild? Like good or bad?"

He reaches over and stops her from moving away, pulling her closer. "What do you think? You're so beautiful."

The reassuring compliment makes her feel better. Her cheeks blush, and she smiles.

Adam's relaxed behavior reminds her that this type of morning event is a regular occurrence. With a final cuddle, he sits on the edge of the bed and stretches his arms above his head. "You want water or coffee or something?"

She takes his offer as an endearing action.

Waiting for her reply, he stands and gathers his clothes from the floor. Quickly he pulls on his boxer briefs.

As he bends down to place his legs through the holes of his jeans, she checks out his body and nods. "That would be nice. I'd like that." Not wanting to be too difficult, she gives an indecisive answer. "Either is fine. I'll just have whatever you're having."

Adam smirks.

Following his lead, Zoe peels the covers away from her body and gets out of bed to fetch her clothes. Unlike with him, it takes her a minute to find all her things. She has no recollection of where she placed them but laughs it off, assuming she was the one who removed them. Playing it cool, she smiles as she puts each item back on her thin frame. While zipping up her skirt, she notices a bruise on her wrist and two larger ones on her thighs. Confused, she makes a joke to cover her nervousness over what her drunk self must have done. "Wow, that's embarrassing. I must have been a real shit show."

As Adam looks over to see what she's referring to, he realizes she has no memory of what transpired last night. As he steps toward her, she shamefully stares at the floor.

Putting on his smolder, he grabs her hands in his and flips the one with the bruise over to examine it. To make it feel better, he kisses the injury. "If you were a shit show, you were the cutest one I've ever seen," he says, spinning the narrative.

She makes eye contact with him and smiles. All the good memories of their time together before she blacked out flood back.

"Come on. Let's get some coffee." He takes her hand and leads her out the bedroom door and down the hall to the staircase.

As they head down the stairs, Zoe scans the living room. Everything appears different from the night before. College students lie passed out in uncomfortable positions, and questionable wreaking puddles scatter the hardwood. Nothing seems glamorous, so she takes a breath, deciding to grow up a little.

Dealing with this every weekend makes the situation appear normal to Adam; the sight of the mess and random individuals doesn't even make him flinch.

Zoe nervously chuckles when they make their way through the archway to the kitchen. "It low-key looks like a zombie apocalypse back there."

Adam laughs at her naivety and blows it off. "Same shit, different weekend."

Zoe shrugs and tightens her grip around his hand.

As his fingers give her three tight squeezes, the ring of a phone cuts the stale beer-infused air. Feeling panic, he releases his grip to pat his jean pocket in search of his cell phone. "What the fuck did I do with it?" he grumbles, then listens for the sound and opens each cabinet to hunt for it.

His search amuses her. Watching him lose something makes her feel less like an alien for not remembering most of the night and also normalizes her behavior.

"I'm sure you think this is hilarious right now," he says.

She shrugs with a laugh. "I mean...it could be worse. At least you have a phone." Realizing he still can't find it, she comes to the rescue to help him look. As he searches the last cabinet, she opens the fridge and rummages inside, following the sound of the ring. Distracted by her mystery-solving focus, Adam sneaks up behind her and wraps his arms around her to hug her waist.

The affection makes Zoe jump at the exact moment she points to the phone, which is hiding behind a case of hard seltzers. "You know they don't go in the fridge, right?"

He beats her to the punch as she reaches to retrieve it and snatches it from the shelf. Frantically he turns the screen away from her view and rapidly scrolls through his missed messages. "Oh, shit," he says as his fingers contact the phone's icy surface.

His reaction fills Zoe with insecurity. "What?" she asks, trying to glance over his shoulder.

Turning the screen to face her, he shrugs with a smile. The photo is the one he posted of them together the night before. "Looks like everyone loves us."

Not remembering the photo being taken, Zoe snatches it from his hands to get a better view.

He laughs at her excitement and swift reaction. "Guess that means you're stuck with me."

She passes the phone back to him with a grin. "Not the worst thing that's happened to me."

Living in the moment, Adam places his phone on the counter, pulls Zoe closer, and rubs her back.

While in his embrace, Zoe spots the time on the digital clock above the stove. "Holy shit! It's ten forty-five already?" After pushing herself away from his chest, she anxiously paces the room.

Finding Zoe's sudden shift in attention toward him off-putting, Adam grabs his phone to receive validation elsewhere. He passively laughs to cover his irritation. "Why the attitude? You have a curfew or something?"

She stops and rolls her eyes. "It's a long fucking story."

Making one last attempt to get some action before she leaves, Adam rushes over and hoists her onto the counter.

They immediately start making out, but she stops him. "You can't distract me. I seriously have to go."

He smirks at his small win and helps her down to the floor. Out of obligation, he reluctantly offers to take her home. "You need a ride?"

Wanting to avoid disclosing that she still lives at home, she plays it cool. "Nope, I'm good. Don't sweat it. I'll take the bus."

Adam sifts through his back pocket, pulls out a twenty-dollar bill from the wad of cash he made from the previous night's transaction, and offers it to her. "I'll always take care of you."

"Such a gentleman." The caring gesture fills her with warmth and sharing a smile with him, she takes the twenty. "Man, last night was so perfect. I don't want to go."

He takes hold of her hands and winks. "Until next time?"

At a loss for words, Zoe looks to the floor and heads to the exit. Stopping for a moment, she turns to face him. "Until next time," she says, then flirtatiously smiles and blows him a kiss.

His hands grasp at the air for the invisible peck. After pretending to catch it, he places it on his cheek.

His reciprocation makes her beam with happiness, and as she exits, she feels like she's floating on a cloud.

The sound of the door shutting signals Adam that the coast is clear, and he immediately scrolls through his social media feed in search of pictures of half-clad women and responds to his plethora of DMs. After exhausting his online options, he pulls up the number from the blonde he met the night before and sends her a smiley-face text. Glancing at the closed door, he chuckles. "Out of sight, out of mind," he gloats.

Chapter Six

YOU CAN'T CATCH ME

Zoe stands facing the street for a moment while enjoying the cool breeze lightly caressing her cheek. Analyzing the twenty-dollar bill in her hand, she smiles at the fact that, for once in her life, a man finally values her. The smile remains etched on her face as she walks with a bounce down the path to the sidewalk.

Oblivious to the trash littering the yard, she turns her steps into joyous skips. She's on cloud nine and nothing can ruin her moment. Halfway down the path, she kicks a plastic cup and does a twirl. "Feels like a dream," she nearly sings. Her lungs release a love-sick sigh. Taking one last look at the cash in her hands, she gives it a quick kiss and stashes it in her pocket. With a giant heave, she exits through the property's gate onto the street. The creak of the ungreased hinges sounds like a merry tune to her ears, and the unconventional music makes her smirk.

She scans both ways down the street, expecting to see Dale's car parked in the same location as the night before. At first glance, she doesn't see it, so she heads down the road, peering down every driveway to make sure it's not hiding in a new spot. This is unusual because, typically, they wait for her to give her a ride home. Not having any luck spotting the car, she gives up. She laughs, deciding the drama surrounding their argument probably distracted them and they forgot she was there. "Good for Britt. Hopefully, she finally got rid of him." Spinning her friend's lack of care into something positive, she shrugs and takes matters into her own hands to find her way home.

Not having made the trek alone before, she uses familiar landmarks and the exterior details of homes to guide her. She hums with each step as she meanders down the empty street. Rather than view this as a walk of shame, she spins it into a fun adventure.

After taking a few turns, both right and wrong, she locates the familiar bus stop in the distance. Slowly making her way toward it, she observes a group of eclectic individuals crowded around an awning-covered bench. She's relieved to see them conversing and laughing. "I'm just in time," she mutters. "Thank God."

The sound of the approaching bus hydraulics cutting through the late-morning air stirs panic in her bones. Knowing the next bus will take at least an hour to arrive, she picks up her pace, then falls into a dead sprint.

One by one, the crowd disappears into the stopped bus. As the last individual goes inside, the driver peers through the open door to see if anyone else remains—it's the same woman from the previous day.

Zoe recognizes the familiar face. "Shit!" she shouts at the stopped bus to stall its departure. "Wait! I'm coming!"

The driver squints through the open door to see who's shouting, and upon seeing her face, she immediately remembers Zoe. "Oh, hell no." Not wanting to deal with another drunken escapade, she quickly pulls the lever to close the door.

Just as Zoe reaches the bus stop, the bus speeds off down the street. She throws her hands up toward the sky in frustration. "You've gotta be kidding me!" Lowering them in defeat, she glimpses her reflection in the plexiglass shelter surrounding the single bench. Her eyeliner, smeared from her having fallen asleep in her full makeup, creates dark shadows under her eyes. She looks a mess between her ripped tights, disheveled clothing, and a multitude of bruises. Irritated at Adam for letting her leave the house looking like a druggy, she turns to face the direction of the departed bus to offload her anger.

Raising her fists, she flips off the world while screaming at the top of her lungs. "You know what? Fuck you! I don't need a ride anyway!" She catches her breath and grumbles, "It's okay. A little walk never hurt anyone." Her Docs lead the way, shuffling beneath her. "Well, can't get any worse, I guess." After a few steps, the laces on her boots become untied and slap against the leather with every stomp. Rolling her eyes, she refrains from admitting her universal defeat by ignoring the inconvenience.

A police vehicle slows its approach, creeping up behind her. The officer behind the wheel witnessed her angry outburst and follows her path to assess the situation. The traditional black-and-white paint perfectly accents the outdated headlight bar and lack of cosmetic upgrades. After following her for half a block, the officer flashes the lights on the top of the car and sounds a bloop of the siren to get her attention.

Being all too familiar with the noise, she stiffens her posture and rolls her eyes. "Seriously?" She approaches a cross street while acting oblivious to her surroundings by pretending to wear earbuds blaring nonexistent music. Zoe swiftly pivots and walks the opposite way, turning her face away from the street and toward a line of brick buildings to shield her identity. *It's cool; just act like everything is cool.* Taking a deep breath, she continues in the wrong direction, adjusts her imaginary earbuds, and plays a set of invisible drums to sell the scenario.

The officer doesn't buy her show and speeds up to catch up with her, then slows the car to match her pace. As the wheels crawl down the pavement beside her, the car's proximity triggers her to ramp up her performance.

The passenger window of the cop car slowly rolls down.

Realizing her efforts to hide are futile, she cuts the act. Reluctantly she turns her body to calmly face the officer.

Sitting in the vehicle's driver's seat is Norm, a forty-year-old male with a dark mustache resembling a well-pruned hedge. He has the standard dark-blue uniform and a buzz-cut with graying sideburns.

To mask her unkempt appearance, Zoe gives a fake smile. "Top of the day to you." After her hands straighten up her tank top, she casually attempts to manipulate her clothing to cover the bruises on her skin and the hole in her tights. Her shoulders shrug. "What seems to be the problem, Officer?"

His tensed jaw quietly chews a piece of gum while he stares at her. Lowering his aviators to the bridge of his nose, he peers over the top, assessing her tattered appearance.

She immediately recognizes him as her uncle, and her demeanor relaxes.

"Looks like you've been drug down a muddy road," he says.

His abrasive comment wipes the smile clean off her face.

"It appears there's a missing teen by the name of Zoe. You happen to have seen her anywhere?"

The corny joke annoys her. Before he can get out a full laugh over her appearance, she sarcastically joins in to overshadow his mockery. At the peak of her hysteria, she silences herself and glares. "Who sent you? Steve?"

With a chuckle, he nods. "You know your dad means well. He's just looking out for you."

Irritated by her uncle Norm's remarks, Zoe turns and storms off. The car follows her, and she angrily stops. Clenching her fists, she turns her body to face the vehicle. She then lets out a deep exhalation to help tame her anger. It doesn't work, and she explodes. "You only say that because he's your brother. Seriously, you don't understand... The guy's a complete asshole!"

Hearing the foul language, he removes his sunglasses. "You gotta cut him some slack. He loved your mother more than anything."

Zoe approaches the open window and places her hands on the car to lean in closer. Seething with pent-up anger, she speaks through her tightly clenched jaw. "It's been five fucking years. Five! Not two, not three! Five!"

Her attitude wears his patience to the width of a razor's edge. Not wanting a confrontation, he hits the button on the side of his door to unlock the car and motions to the backseat for her to get in.

In an act of defiance, she crosses her arms and plants her feet.

Her uncle's face is stern. "I don't want to do this the hard way, so just get in the back, Zoe."

As she takes a moment to weigh her options, she remembers the last time she chose not to comply.

⇒⇒ ⋅⊹⋅ ⇐⇐

It was a night to remember or, in her case, forget. Roughly two months ago, the evening's weather was warmer than usual after the football game. All the players and fans fled home, except Zoe, who stayed behind to watch the moon and stars set over the high school stadium. The floodlights surrounding the field provided competition to their twinkle as she waited for the janitor to flip the switch to "off." Gearing up for the last lights to fade to black, she chugged several cans of beer she swiped from her father's fridge earlier that day.

She didn't consider that the lighting would remain on for security and that the expected outcome would never happen. After she chugged the eighth can, her skin felt like a furnace, and she stripped down to her bra and underwear to compensate. Like clockwork, the school's security cameras detected a partially clad, intoxicated young woman on the monitoring system.

If sitting in the stands half naked wasn't bad enough, she passed the time by taking laps around the field with her backpack full of beer.

Her uncle was the first to respond. Recognizing Zoe, he tried to save her embarrassment by giving her a verbal warning. Standing at the top of the steps leading down to the field, he shouted for her to put *her clothes on. "The shows over, kid. Put your clothes on, and I'll give you a ride home."*

His forceful voice caught her attention. She stared at him, stuck out her tongue, and hysterically laughed. Without warning, she bolted across the turf.

"Jesus Christ." Having no other option, Norm raced down the steep steps and hopped the short chain link fence to chase her down.

Her attempt felt like a game, so she ran faster, mocking him with her slurred speech. The act of throwing empty beer cans from her backpack over her shoulder, intending to slow him down, added to the ridiculous visual. "Stop fucking chasing me; it's after school hours!" Her staggering jog turned into a skip. As she glanced behind her, his heavy breathing made her laugh. "I can do what I want. This is public prop-erty!" Feeling invincible, she drove her point home by flipping him off with both hands. She then turned her body and jogged backward to give him the best view of the gesture. She drunkenly lost footing, however, and tumbled ass over teakettle onto the grass.

Norm raced over and handcuffed her.

"Fuck," she slurred, her face smashed into the turf.

»»—•—««

The memory of waking up in a jail cell the next day with a massive bruise on her face from the drunken fall is enough to convince her to get in the vehicle. With an enormous sigh, she climbs into the back of the car and shuts the door behind her. She peers out the window to watch the moving scenery, then glances at her uncle's reflection in the rearview mirror and shrugs. "Well, at least it's a free ride."

He takes a moment to collect himself to have a serious talk. Meeting her gaze in the silver-backed glass, he clears his throat to speak. "You know, it doesn't have to be this way."

Assuming the conversation will be a lecture, Zoe avoids it and pretends to be distracted by staring out the backseat window.

He knows a reality check is the only way to get through to her. "You look like shit." Immediately, he glances in the mirror to see her reaction.

The comment irritates her, and she rolls her eyes. "Let's cut the crap. How did you manage to find me anyway?"

Her reaction confirms that she's listening, so he continues. "You can thank your new boyfriend. He gave your location away when he posted that picture of the two of you on his social media. The station got word of his party happening about a week ago, and we've been tracking him since the tip-off."

"Hmm," she replies, blaming her uncle Norm for ruining her life's one happy moment.

"So when your dad filed another missing person report for you, I connected the dots." He chuckles at the stupidity of not covering her tracks when trying to run away. "I'm not a moron like you think I am."

Zoe is more irritated that he may mess up her dating life than she is over the fact that he caught her. Crossing her arms stresses her angry pout, making her unhappiness clear. "Of course, as soon as one good thing finally happens in my life, you ruin it!" She uncrosses her arms and sarcastically gives a round of applause. "Good for you!"

Norm pulls the car up to the station, puts it in park, and flips the ignition key to the left. Everything falls silent, and he turns to face her. Concern sets into his expression as he peers through the plexiglass divider.

Avoiding eye contact, she stares out the window.

His demeanor shifts to a more serious tone. "I'm worried about you, Zoe. You being my favorite—well, only—niece, I feel we need to cut the shit before we go inside. That photo Adam posted last night had cocaine in the background. Since the police already have issued a warrant for you, I have no choice but to take you in."

She doesn't want to acknowledge the facts.

He glances toward the station. "The court won't be as forgiving on your third possession charge. When you face the judge, you'll have two options: incarceration or institutional rehab as a plea deal. You need to take the deal."

The word *rehab* disgusts her. Her jaw clenches as she glares at him in disbelief. "I'm not an addict—"

Tired of her bullshit, he interjects. "Cut the crap, kid. Just take the plea when it's offered. You aren't cut out for jail, and since your mom had some priors, it'll be easy to get the judge on your side."

She scoots her body to the edge of her seat to deliver her response. "If it gets you to shut up, fine, I'll take the fucking plea deal—just let me out of the car. It smells like piss in here."

Zoe's uncle smiles, believing he's finally gotten through to her. With a quick nod, he hops out of the car to get her.

Feeling like her world is ending, she seethes. She then lets out a loud grunt and slams her head into the divider separating the front and back seats. The force of the impact makes her blackout.

Chapter Seven

THIS MUST BE HELL

March 2015, Rehab

Wafts of the synthetic thick blue sheets and medical-grade gloves' strong odors travel through the ventilation system and into the confines of each room. The walls all appear the same, eggshell white, while the floors are a dusty cream.

Pharmaceutical sedation compounds Zoe's lethargy from being knocked out cold. The fluorescent lights above antagonize the throbbing sensation radiating from inside her skull. She leaves her eyes tightly closed to avoid looking directly at the harsh illumination. As she squirms to get comfortable under the stiff sheets, she hears something rustling in the hallway. It sounds like squeaks from someone scribbling on a classroom whiteboard.

As she wakes up a bit more, her ears differentiate an additional sound echoing between the icy walls and the tiled floor: a muddied steady beep. As she focuses on guessing what object is creating the sound, another round of sharp jabbing sensations hits her skull. She moans at the pain. "Am I in hell?" she cries.

She draws in a deep breath to help take the edge off the ache. As she releases the heavy exhalation, her left hand migrates to feel the injury on her head. Only making it a few inches away from her side, she finds something has limited her limb's range of motion. Frustrated, she gives a hefty tug and is met by a rug-burn sensation against her wrist.

If there's one thing Zoe doesn't like, it's situations that trigger her claustrophobia. Her greatest fear is being controlled, and the inability to move freely makes her feel trapped. She panics. As her heart races, she tries to move her opposite hand and encounters the same resistance. Trying to stop a panic attack from ensuing, she wiggles each of her legs, hoping the freedom of her two lower limbs will make her feel less confined. When she finds each ankle trapped the same way, her mind spins. Her escalated heart rate exacerbates her throbbing headache, and her eyes fly open. *This can't be happening.* She stares up at the popcorn ceiling and into the dreadful light that blazes so brightly it penetrates her soul. Her eyes frantically dart around the room. She tries shifting her head right to left to expand her view and realizes a neck brace limits her mobility. *What the fuck is going on?*

Having watched too many psychological thrillers, she immediately concludes that someone has kidnapped her. Paranoia heightens her anxiety, and each breath becomes quicker than the last as she tugs at the constraints. She fights to grasp a deep breath to magnify her shout. "Help!" she screams. Every bit of her skin weirdly combines clamminess with beads of sweat. Flailing again, she panics. "Help, help. I'm trapped!"

Her pupils shift cross-eyed as she strains to look toward the end of the bed at her toes partially sticking out from under the rigid fabric. Shaking her knees to edge off the single sheet covering her, she notices an unfamiliar outfit made up of beige slipper socks, a wife beater, and gray sweatpants.

A new piece of jewelry adorns her wrist: a plastic hospital band.

Scanning the room with her limited view and a bit more clarity, she sees the upper half of the walls painted in neutral, non-stimulating colors. Besides her reclining prison, only one piece of furniture is positioned next to her in the sterile space: a desk. Its minimalist appearance houses clean carved lines of orange-tinged wood.

Pushing her neck brace to its limits, Zoe grunts as she rotates her head to the right. As she gains the willpower to move past the constraint, she observes a whiteboard heavily secured midway up the granola-decorated wall.

The writing across the top reads: *Zoe—NA, AAA, ED, SW, Flight Risk.* Next to the words is a smiley face doodle.

She cringes at the lengthy handwritten list.

⊰⊱•⊰⊱

Oh, fuck. I'm in hell after all.

⊰⊱•⊰⊱

Another wave of pain rolls through her skull, making her eyes roll, and a separate gnawing ache stemming from her tongue accompanies it. Wanting to reminisce about the single good time with her crush, she opens her mouth to spin the barbell against her teeth but finds her jewelry is gone, and she is left with nothing but a sore tongue. The thought that this place won't let her have a single moment of joy angers her. Fighting the restraints, she flicks off the heart monitor from her right index finger, causing the rhythmic sound of the machine to flatline.

The abrupt shift in her vitals triggers an alarm, sending emergency code messages over the intercom system.

To tune out the aggressive noise, she focuses on the ceiling. Suddenly she hears the door swing open and the sound of running footsteps approaching. Every second that passes, the chaotic clamber grows louder, and each audible noise, once classified as ambiance, amplifies in her eardrums. All she wants to do is cover her ears with her hands, but she can't. As her panic heightens, her clothing becomes drenched in a pool of sweat and her body compulsively shakes. Her teeth chatter between her lips, her eyes darting as they strain to catch sight of the approaching body. The hazy image of a nurse enters her field of view.

Rushing to her side, the nurse checks her vitals. Her lungs release a sigh of relief upon hearing the steady beat of Zoe's heart through the stethoscope. Quickly, she turns to ask a question. "Can you tell me your name?"

Although annoyed, she still answers. "Zoe."

Smiling, the nurse nods. "Good."

"Can you tell me why I'm here, chained to the bed?" Zoe asks.

"Well, you hit your head pretty hard, giving you a nice little goose egg. When you were taken to the hospital, they contacted your dad since you were a minor. He opted for you to be transferred to rehab." She reaches for the bandage on Zoe's head and checks the injured area underneath. "Looking much better."

The room's air against the wound makes her wince. "Jeez, watch it." Shaking the bindings to garner sympathy, she seizes the opportunity to ask to be freed from her restraints. "Is it possible to let me out of these things?"

The woman leans forward and softens her expression as she assesses the risk factor of releasing her. "Usually I wouldn't do that, but I'll make an exception since you have a hard road ahead." As she unfastens the buckles, her speech picks up pace. "But don't try anything. I don't want to send Tom, the lead nurse, down here to sedate you."

Feeling the last restraint undone, Zoe rubs the skin on her raw wrist and nods. "Isn't your job supposed to be uplifting? What do you mean by 'hard road'?" She tilts her head to take in the nurse's appearance and notices she's already across the room, writing on the whiteboard.

She points to the name she's written. "I'm Stacy."

As Zoe thinks of a sarcastic rebuttal, her body suffers minor seizures and sweat pours from her skin. Immediately her eyes scan the room for help.

Catching her building panic from the corner of her eye, Stacy turns to her. "Small seizures are completely normal when you detox. You just have to ride the wave. It'll all be over soon enough."

Zoe's shaking becomes uncontrollable. She tries to calm her spasmodic pain by curling into a ball. As her eyeliner streams down her cheeks like a river of tar, she huddles drenched in sweat in a fetal position. The pain becomes so excruciating that she screams.

The nurse rushes to comfort her. As she places her hand on her back, the teenager swats it away.

"Don't touch me, you fat-ass bitch!"

Familiar with the process, nurse Stacy recoils her hand and takes a step back. "I'll just leave you to it then." Though she's witnessed the effects of detox many times before, she's still a bit shaken by Zoe's hurtful words. She takes a moment to regain her composure before making her way to the room's exit. Upon reaching the door, she turns and smiles at Zoe. "I'll come back to check on you."

Irritated by her lingering presence, she yells louder. "Leave!"

Stacy scampers outside and quietly closes the door.

Seconds turn to minutes, minutes to hours, hours to days, and days to weeks. Although she has experienced times of defeat, every moment that passes seems more bearable than the last.

Chapter Eight

NO ONE CARES, LULU

One Month Later, Rehab

Muted shouts echo off the hospital walls outside Zoe's room. Nervously sitting on the edge of her freshly made twin bed, she stares at the new writing added to the fixed whiteboard across the room. *Time sure flies.* She picks at the hospital band still around her wrist. Her comfortable attire is the same but clean, and her skin is clear of any remnants of makeup. Dark circles rest beneath her eyes and her frame appears frailer than when she arrived because she barely ate during her weeks of detox.

A bird chirps from outside the window, and Zoe shifts the position of her body to look. Even though she's come to accept her current situation, she still has some fight left inside and resents the way they forcefully checked her into the facility. She walks to the window to see the sun shining onto the green lawn below. Her finger taps the glass to get the bird's attention. "They don't know how easy they have it. I didn't sign up for this shit." The sight of them makes her think of life outside of the facility. In the middle of her daydream, she hears the door open and, without turning, shouts, "Good morning, Stacy!"

The nurse enters the room smiling from ear to ear. "I see someone's up early this morning."

Her chipper attitude is off-putting to Zoe. Keeping her back turned, she makes a disgusted face, mocking the woman.

Stacy races across the room to place a medication cup on the desk next to Zoe's bed. With each jolly step, her perfectly rolled bangs bounce, while the material of her pastel blue scrubs creates static sounds.

Hearing the wax-coated Dixie cup hit the top of the wooden surface prompts Zoe to relive the chalky texture and foul taste of the medication in her mouth. The experience makes her shoulders shudder. Refraining from turning away from the window, she uses a cheery voice to pretend she's clueless about what the nurse is doing behind her. "What's it now, Stacy?"

Staring at her lean back, the woman answers in an equally cheery tone. "Today is the day you get phone benefits! I know how much you've been looking forward to that."

To hide her reaction, she continues to gaze at the birds. A smile takes over her lips for the first time in a while. "Now we're talking, Stacy!" Immediately her mind runs through a list of individuals she can call.

The nurse allows Zoe a moment of excitement before revealing the catch. Wasting no time, she picks up the cup of pills from the table and shakes the contents like a maraca. "You just have to do one thing: take your medication."

The stipulation wipes the smile from Zoe's face, and her moment of happiness wanes. Slowly she turns around to express her disappointment. "People would like you more if there wasn't always a fucking catch."

With the medication cup in her grasp, her shoulders shrug as her feet walk toward Zoe. "Well, it's my job to get you to feel better, and the medication goes hand in hand with that."

Rolling her eyes, Zoe knows what she must do and extends her hand. Stacy pours the assortment of pills into her palm, and on reflex, she pops them into her mouth. Her eyes close as she swallows, and she sticks her tongue out to show they're gone. With her mouth gaping open, she speaks in a mocking tone. "You happy now?"

The nurse smiles and nods.

Zoe's eyes roll with irritation. "Now, can I have my phone time?"

Stacy walks across the room to toss the cup in the trash and motions for her to follow. Not wanting to miss her opportunity, Zoe sprints to catch up and accompanies her out the exit.

The hallway is bustling with random nursing staff going from room to room. An endless row of rectangular fluorescent lights guides their way down the long white-walled corridor. The lighting in the hall seems much brighter than in her quarters, and she shields her eyes from the overwhelming glare.

Zoe speeds up her pace to catch up while scanning the patients' names listed on each entry she passes. It surprises her that there doesn't appear to be a single unoccupied space, and she chuckles. "Full house, huh?"

With her focus solely on transferring her from point a to b without incident, Stacy's mind doesn't have time to process her joke, and she ignores her.

Irritated by the lack of response, Zoe gives up on making small talk and crosses her arms with a pout. "Cool."

They reach a wooden door with a grated window at the end of their lengthy walk.

Immediately Zoe notices that, unlike the rest of the doors, this one doesn't have an individual's name labeling it. Instead, it has a metal sign that reads, media room.

"All right, here we are," Stacy quickly chatters. She peers through the window to see if anyone is inside, then takes a set of keys from her pocket to unlock the entrance. As she opens the heavy door, it triggers the automatic fluorescent overhead lights to turn on. She gestures for Zoe to enter. "After you."

Concerned she might miss her opportunity or they'll revoke her privilege, she springs inside. Immediately upon passing through the entry, she peers around the room to assess her surroundings.

On the far side of the beige-colored space sits a faux wood Formica-topped counter and three metal foldout chairs. Three old push-button phones rest an equal distance apart on the cream-colored surface. Short dividers made from large pieces of brown cardboard separate the telephones to give a false sense of privacy. The wall to the left of the phones has three old computers collecting dust on a second matching tabletop.

Zoe rushes in a dead sprint toward the modern-day lifelines. Before she can pick which one to use, the nurse shouts to get her attention and explain the rules. "Not so fast! Since this is your first time here, we must review the guidelines!"

Her feet stop, and she reluctantly turns to listen.

"Very good. So you only get ten minutes of monitored phone or computer time. I reiterate that everything is monitored, so absolutely no funny business." She points to the cameras in the upper corners of the drab space.

Not wanting to waste a single second of her ten-minute allotment, Zoe agrees.

"I'll leave you to it," Stacy states as she exits.

The sound of the door shutting serves as Zoe's start time, and she rushes to the phone positioned farthest from the hallway.

As her fingers excitedly dial a number, the nurse watches her through the grates.

Hearing the ring through the receiver escalates her anticipation, and she nervously taps her foot against the tiled floor. "Come on, come on, come on... Pick up." Still waiting for someone to answer, she nervously glances at the window to see if Stacy is still staring and is uncomfortable after verifying that she is, in fact, intently watching her. Trying to preserve her privacy, she shifts forward in her seat to hide behind the flimsy divider.

At the same time, Zoe's fingers frantically tap the counter; Britt is apathetically on the receiving end of the chiming rings. Using her phone's front-facing camera to apply a third coat of bubble-gum pink glitter lip gloss, she glances at the call notification and sees "No Caller ID" across the top of her screen. Her toes wiggle while she bobs to the beat of the music, showcasing her black furry slip-on slides, zebra-print biker shorts, and matching bra top. The volume of the ring, however, is unavoidable. After watching videos detailing her favorite celebrity gossip, she had forgotten to turn her sound back down from its highest setting. She lies carefree on her pink furry blanket draped across her bed in her room's cozy confinements. A boombox with a built-in alarm clock sits on a chestnut-colored dresser with bedazzled crystal knobs and blares the newest pop song. Britt squints again to read the notification related to the incoming call. The ugly sound of the ring inconveniences her, so she jumps off the bed to turn up the stereo and drown out the sound.

The phone continues to ring.

Finally, Britt slams her tube of gloss down next to the blaring boombox. "Ugh, so annoying!" she squeals. As her finger moves to reject the call, she thinks about not having heard from Dale in a few days and thinks it might be him. Unwilling to miss an opportunity to argue, she coyly smirks and pushes the "answer" button. Before speaking a single word, she flips the conversation to the speakerphone and twists the stereo's knob to turn down the music. Ready to offload her petty irritation on the interrupting caller, her voice loudly clears to build anticipation for her wrath of sarcasm. "You've reached Britt. Who the hell is this?"

There's no human response to her greeting, only static.

Convinced Dale is playing a prank on her, she walks across the room and grabs a bottle of Barbie-pink nail polish from her nightstand drawer. Even though he can't see what she's doing, she's learned from watching teen romance movies that pampering yourself while conversing with a boy you're upset with reads as hard to get. With her nail polish in hand, she tosses the cell phone onto the bed, flops next to it, and begins painting her nails. The phone's silence frustrates her and makes her sassier. "Um, hello?" she snaps.

Hearing her best friend's voice brings a tremendous sense of relief to Zoe, putting a smile on her face. It's been a month since she's spoken to anyone outside the facility. The moment becomes overwhelming, and she finds herself at a loss for words. Knowing Britt's lack of patience, she squirms in her seat, concerned that she'll hang up because of the delay. Finally, she gathers a reply and responds in a tone that matches Britt's sarcastic energy. "Who the fuck do you think this is?" she yells loudly, with unconstrained excitement. Concerned she might have attracted unwanted attention, she glances toward to door with paranoia and catches Stacy still glaring at her through the window.

The sound of Zoe's feminine voice causes some disappointment. Giving herself a moment to put on a chipper tone, Britt answers with a fake happy timbre. "Oh, my God! Zoe?! Where have you been?" she asks, holding up her hand to admire her polished fingers.

Excited to commiserate, Zoe rapidly begins updating her on the situation. "You won't..." She pauses mid-sentence, startled by the sound of the door being opened to the media room. Worried Stacy is coming to get her, she freezes and whispers into the receiver, "Hold on one sec." As her upper body turns to look, her hand covers the mouthpiece to mute it.

A male nurse with a dark-brown mustache and thick glasses escorts another female patient into the room for media privileges. Once she's fully inside, he says, "Okay, Lulu, you have ten minutes and no funny business this time." He steps back out to the hallway and shuts the door.

The incoming teenager appears to be around Zoe's age and wears the same light-gray sweats, but hers are dirty. Her over-processed bleached hair is dry as a bone; the only moisture is the greasy shine. The whites of her eyes are somewhat dark as they sit in the gaunt sunken holes above her high-set cheekbones. She scans the room to state her dominance and meets Zoe's glare. Immediately she clenches her fists and stomps her foot. "What are you staring at, twizzle dick?" she asks.

The insult makes Zoe's jaw tighten. Strategically using her opposite hand, she shields her middle finger from the staff to flip her off.

The girl laughs at the attempted rebuttal. As the teen walks past the row of telephones, she ignores Zoe's gesture. Not wanting to miss her media time, she hustles to sit at a computer directly opposite her.

Hearing the perturbing girl push back the metal legs of her chair against the cold tile triggers her anxiety. Instantly, her emotions flip from angst to remorse, not for doing the action but for wasting her precious allocated ten minutes of time. With the phone still in her hand, she holds it away from her ear and peers back at the window to see if Stacy caught the encounter.

She sighs in relief upon seeing the hospital workers distracted, engrossed in a playful conversation sparked by Stacy's blatant flirtation with the male nurse. The thirty-five-year-old-or-so man coyly brushes his thick mustache with his fingers. His hand position and deepened exhalations cause his thick glasses to fog. Their matching muted-colored blue scrubs make them resemble a couple attending a costume party.

The sight of them comingling disgusts Zoe, and in an attempt not to throw up, she turns her upper body back around in the makeshift cubicle to mind her own business. After lightly clearing her throat, she lifts the receiver back to her ear to talk to her friend.

Little did Zoe know that when all the commotion began, Britt muted her phone due to her lack of interest in conversing and to avoid distraction from her life's priorities, which encompassed applying a second coat of nail polish. Waving her wet nails into the air to get them to dry, she smirks at how unique the sparkle of the polish looks in the light. The sound of her friend's breath projecting through the phone ruins the moment, however, and she apathetically taps the mute button with her index finger to fulfill her obligation. Feeling their conversation no longer serves her, she hurries it along so she can get on with her day of pampering.

"Who was that?" she asks. Waiting for the response, she continues to blow on her fingers to dry the lacquer faster.

Zoe turns to see if the patient typing away on the computer behind her is listening. Seeing the coast is clear, she swiftly cups her hand around the mouthpiece to shield her conversation. Taking her secretive nature an extra step, she shifts her body to lean forward over the table between the dividers and picks up the chat pace. "Uh, it doesn't matter; I have to talk fast. I only have a few minutes," she says. Her eyes shut as she relives how she ended up in rehab. Everything surrounding that night triggers something inside her, the memories sending a shiver of anxiety down her spine. "That morning after Adam's party, I was minding my business, just walking home, when a cop car pulled up beside me... I swear the thing came out of nowhere..."

The company in the room continues to be distracted, mindlessly clicking on her computer's keyboard as she plays a game of *Pac-Man*.

As she recounts the event, each sound of the keys clicks, adding another chip to her building anxiety.

During Zoe's rendition of the traumatizing story, Britt is multitasking. She takes a selfie, edits its, posts it on her social media, and revels in the number of likes and the names of her admirers as they trickle in. She gasps. Trix likes her photo, and she's in disbelief. "No!" she yelps.

Believing her friend's lengthy gasp relates to her story about running into the cop, Zoe continues. "Those assholes gave me the option of juvie or three months in rehab. I'm sure you can guess which one I chose," she says.

Even though the patient behind her is playing a series of video games, she makes it obvious she's been eavesdropping and interjects a comment to chime in. "She's a dumbass if she didn't guess re hab... You don't get the phone privileges this early in juvie. I should know," she states with a snicker.

Zoe rolls her eyes at the unsolicited opinion. Covering the bottom mouthpiece, she shifts her head and glares at the girl. "Don't you have anything better to do?"

Lulu continues playing her game on the computer and shrugs.

She removes her hand from the receiver and redirects her attention to the phone call.

Britt continues to halfheartedly listen while blowing on her nails to speed up the air-dry of her polish. Though she doesn't care to hear the story of how Zoe ended up in confinement, the sound of her friend bantering with someone else makes her jealous. "You'd better not be replacing me with a new bestie," she says.

The thought of befriending the obnoxious girl sitting behind her makes her laugh. "With these trash buckets? No, thank you. I'd rather die than be that desperate."

Hearing that her friend's loyalty hasn't changed, even after she abandoned Zoe at the party, makes her smirk. Knowing there's no way of being released early, Britt offers her a ride to reciprocate the bond. "So should I come and spring you out?"

Zoe sighs with disappointment, the thought of getting out making her daydream for a moment. "I wish! Thank God I only have two more months in this hellhole."

She places the nail polish back on her nightstand as she listens to the timeline of her release. Suddenly she gets an idea. "Wait—two months?" she asks.

"Yup," Zoe says as she scans the window leading to the hallway.

Stacy gives her direct eye contact and taps her wrist to signal that time is running out.

"Yay, we can still go to that music fest then?" Britt asks. Even though she invited many individuals to attend the event, she wants to ensure she has a backup just in case the others fall through.

Zoe's eyes light up with the thought of having something to look forward to. "Holy fuck, yes!" she says with a huge smile. "It's definitely the silver lining for this whole thing."

Britt claps her hands and squeals with superficial excitement. Having regained the emotional dependency she craves, she continues with her manipulative scheme, adding more points to the conversation that she knows will interest her. "You know, I heard through the grapevine that Adam is supposed to be there."

The sound of her crush's name makes Zoe nervous, and she compulsively bites her nails. "Has he asked about me?" she inquires.

Knowing the honest answer may change her compliant attitude, Britt opens the social media page on her phone and scrolls through his feed, searching for anything that will seal the deal. Photo after photo slides across her screen of him partying with other girls, and the picture posted with Zoe is gone.

She fakes her excitement as she lies through her teeth. "Of course! Oh, my God! How often do I have to tell you the guy is literally in love with you?"

Unable to contain her elation over the validation that her crush is waiting for her return, she jumps in her seat.

Britt continues to silently scroll through Adam's social media feed. Thinking he's hot and knowing he's single, she double taps a few of his pictures to "heart" them.

Stacy raps on the window to signal that Zoe's time is up.

With the handset held to her ear, Zoe swivels to look at her. "Oh, shit. The Wicked Witch of the West flew in on her broom to kick me off the phone," she says with a sigh. Her body straightens, and she clears her throat to get her last words out. "No matter what happens, Britt, I swear things will be back to normal by the time the music fest happens."

A screen notification of an incoming call distracts Britt. Wanting to answer, she makes a kissing sound into the phone to wrap up their conversation. "Oh, Dale is calling! Gotta go. Love you, bitch!"

"Right back—" She encounters the sound of a dial tone mid-sentence. Zoe is pissed, but instead of blaming her friend for the disconnected line, she blames the nurse. She turns around in her seat and sees Stacy waiting behind her. "You have to be shitting me, Stacy," she says, rolling her eyes.

The nurse cuts off her backtalk. "I don't need the sass, Zoe. You know the rules. Ten minutes is ten minutes."

Still irritated about the conversation's abrupt end, Zoe grumbles to show her disdain.

With her many years working in the field of rehabilitation, Stacy is used to dealing with challenging personalities, and Zoe's behavior doesn't faze her. She smiles and extends her hand to help her hang up the phone. "You should thank me. Technically I gave you an extra minute," she says.

Sarcastically bowing, she thanks her. "Or would you prefer me to kiss your feet?" she asks as she makes her way to the floor.

The stunned nurse grabs her by the arm to get her to stand.

Hearing the commotion, Lulu spins around in her chair and laughs. "I need popcorn for this," she says, snickering.

Stacy glares back at her. "Lulu, don't be an instigator." Regaining her composure, she turns to face her assigned patient. "Come on, Zoe. It's time to return to your room."

As the nurse tugs on her arm, Zoe's opinion of the other patient shifts, and she quickly acknowledges her with a smile. The gesture makes Lulu chuckle, and she shakes her head with disbelief.

The nurse forcefully leads Zoe to the hallway and shuts the door to the media room. While gripping her arm, she uses her free hand to motion for Lulu's nurse to walk closer, so she can fill him in on the encounter.

Confident she's trying to get his attention for flirtatious reasons, he eagerly makes his way to her.

Her upper body leans toward him, and she lowers her voice. "FYI, I think you should know Lulu is acting up again," she says.

His face appears disappointed as his eyes dart to the room's window. "Understood," he says. As he reaches for the doorknob to the media room, he turns back to Stacy and winks. "We still on for five thirty tonight?"

It flusters her to talk about her personal life at work, and the question causes her to blush and her lips to smirk. "Of course," she replies. To avoid further embarrassment, she quickly turns and walks down the hall. Realizing the teen lags behind, she signals for her to speed up, and Zoe obliges.

She views the moment as an opportunity to get back at her for messing up her phone time. Her right eye obnoxiously winks at Stacy, mocking the gesture made by the male nurse. "So, is that a thing?" she asks. When she doesn't receive a response, she digs deeper to push her buttons. "Are you guys fucking?"

The nurse ignores her as she frantically fumbles for the keys to unlock Zoe's room.

Noticing the last comment rattled Stacy, Zoe dramatically crosses her arms and impatiently taps her foot.

Stacy's fingers twist the knob, and she turns to address her. "Not appropriate," she says. Fed up with her behavior, she authoritatively points inside as she opens the door. "Go!"

The harsh tone makes Zoe roll her eyes. Uncrossing her arms, she releases a huff of air and drags her feet inside. As she spins around to offer one last remark, the door slams shut in her face. "Geez! You could have broken my nose!" she says as she rubs her nonexistent injury. Receiving little or no rise for her dramatic behavior perturbs her. Pacing the room to pass the time, she counts the tiles on the floor and combs through her thoughts regarding her conversation with Britt. *They won't break me,* she reminds herself for the hundredth time.

Chapter Nine

UGH, THERAPY

Two months have passed since Zoe's glorious arrival, and the whiteboard in the room that tracks her progress reminds her of that. Now two smiley faces are next to her name. Unlike the first, which was standard, the newest one has a stuck-out tongue and an enormous set of eyelashes. Stacy has replaced the number one that was once in the upper right-hand corner with a bubble letter two. The room, now a bit more decorated than when she first arrived, gives the space a bit more of a homey feel.

Over the time Zoe has spent in confinement, she's discovered she has a knack for drawing and painting. Many hand-drawn illustrations encapsulate abstract strokes of grunge themes with a vintage twist. A few sport splashes of color, but most have gray and black hues. She prefers to reflect on her real-life struggles and ongoing turmoil through her artwork. She sits on the end of her bed wearing an oversize gray sweater with black leggings, fuzzy striped socks, and camel-colored slides. Her body is still thin, but her face is no longer gaunt, and her skin appears healthier, with rosy cheeks. Never having been sober for so long since she was a child makes her anxious. To pass the time, she stares at each tiny detail in the red-themed bouquet sitting on her nightstand. Initially, they came in a glass vase, but Stacy transferred them into a plastic container due to the suicide watch they placed her under upon her arrival.

Tucked inside the cluster of flowers is an unopened card peeking out from behind a red rose. She stares at the bouquet, counting each petal and leaf while trying to convince herself to open the card. A loud knock on the door disrupts her thoughts, causing her attention to shift toward the entrance. She smiles at the sight of Stacy poking her head into the room.

The nurse smiles back. "Today's a big day!" she says, shutting the door behind her. "You've been doing great in your recovery, Zoe."

She isn't used to having someone compliment her, so the feeling makes her uncomfortable. As she watches her positive attitude approach from across the room, she masks her lack of self-worth with sarcasm. "Aw, does that mean you're proud of me?" she asks.

Ignoring the remark, Stacy leaves the smile plastered on her face and races over to admire the flowers. As she tilts her head to smell them, she playfully gives Zoe a wink to redirect her thoughts. "These are gorgeous! Who are they from? A secret admirer?"

Realizing what the nurse is trying to do, Zoe has a little fun with the question rather than fighting it. She readjusts her posture to sit on her hands and laughs with a joking shrug. "You know, some people have fetishes for girls stuck in rehab," she states.

Stacy's eyes widen at her response. Nothing surprises her, however, and the specific comment raises concern even though she has seen it all.

Several years prior, the facility had an issue with a creep communicating with a patient. The nurse's posture straightens up, and her demeanor becomes serious.

Reading her tension, Zoe jumps up from the bed. "Jesus, I'm just kidding!" she says, snatching the card from the arrangement. Waving it in front of Stacy's face, she fans the air to help bring color back to her pale complexion. "I don't have to open it to know who sent it. I'd recognize the handwriting on the envelope from anywhere. See the curls at the end of the letter *Z?* My uncle Norm fucking sent them. When I stayed with him for a short stint, I got pretty good at copying his writing to forge notes for school." She then shrugs and anxiously giggles. Holding the envelope to eye level, she purses her lips. "Guess he doesn't hate me as much as I thought he did, even with all the messed-up stuff I've put him through."

Stacy notices Zoe beating herself up over her rocky past, so she takes a step closer and places a hand on her shoulder to comfort her. Looking her in the eyes, she uses a somber tone to reiterate her worth. "You have people who love and care about you, Zoe," she says. "I know you don't believe this, but you're one of the lucky ones. Many recovering addicts who come here never experience what it feels like to have someone on the outside care about them."

Zoe has never really thought about it in those terms before. The revelation causes her to stare down at the floor's tile as she tries to avoid feeling uncomfortable from stirred emotions. She gives a nod of understanding. "I know. "

The nurse gently places her other hand on her opposite shoulder to ensure she has her full attention. "And you deserve it," she states.

Zoe shifts her gaze to the window and laughs as she shimmies Stacy's hands off her shoulders. "Okay, okay. Enough of this sappy shit." Zoe turns and paces the room to redirect her spiraling thoughts. "What's on the agenda today? You're here a lot earlier than usual."

As she gives the teen a moment to calm down, she reaches into the front pocket of her scrubs and pulls out a sealed cup containing her pills. Holding them in the air, she gives them a light shake to get her attention, then sets them next to the flowers.

The sound causes Zoe's pacing feet to stop, and her eyes reluctantly look back at the nurse.

To help lighten the mood and offset her displeasure, Stacy changes her demeanor to one of delight. She raises her hands and wiggles her fingers as if making a celebratory announcement. "It's therapy day!" she says.

Her outlandish attempt to make the news sound appealing doesn't work; Zoe shows her lack of enthusiasm by crossing her arms and planting her feet. "You're kidding, right?" she asks, her voice exuding annoyance.

Stacy tries to erase her negative outlook by reminding her of prior experiences. "Come on; it'll be fun. Think about it... This will be a piece of cake compared to what you went through when you first arrived."

The comparison works, and though still a bit disgruntled, she shrugs in agreement. "I don't know about fun, but I'm sure it can't be as bad as detox," she states. An icy shiver runs down her spine as her mind relives the horrid moments of feeling like she was going to die. As the memory dissipates, she smirks and walks toward the pills. "So when's therapy?" she asks. After opening the cup, she empties the contents into her mouth and closes her eyes to swallow.

With the speed of pulling off a Band-Aid, Stacy races to the door, then turns back to Zoe. "Right now," she replies with a smile.

Clenching her jaw, Zoe chuckles and shakes her head.

"Of course it is," she says with a smirk. Eager for any reason to leave the room, she willingly walks toward the nurse. "Lead the way!"

Stacy doesn't care if the happiness is genuine; she's just pleased with Zoe's unusual compliance with the treatment. "That's the spirit! Here we go," she states, opening the door and rapidly ushering her to the hall.

They walk down the familiar corridor, and like clockwork, Zoe scans the names written on the small whiteboards outside each patient's door. Seeing that one room is empty jostles her usual routine. She's never seen a single name change in all the time she's been there, and it bothers her that someone left before her. A burgeoning idea quickly overshadows the jealousy she feels. To cover her underlying motives and envy, she motions to the door with her thumb and chuckles. "Cheryl finally sprung herself out of here, huh?"

Stacy glances at the blank board and shakes her head. Already one step ahead of her, she responds, "No, you can't change room locations." Without a single break in her step, she continues to walk down the hall.

Perplexed by Stacy beating her to the punch, Zoe stubbornly plants her feet and refuses to follow. Still not getting the attention she seeks, she dramatically throws her hands up, then points to the vacant room. "Come on! Everyone knows it has the best view in this entire joint," she says, ridiculously flailing her arms to enhance her point. "So unfair."

Being forced to deal with Zoe's daily theatrics, Stacy has learned how to squash her outbursts before they escalate. The nurse calmly stops and turns to face her with a frozen blank stare.

Realizing she isn't playing along with her charade, Zoe walks faster to catch up and shifts the conversation. "You know, no one liked Cheryl anyway... I mean, so I've been told," she says with a shrug. She continues to talk as she approaches and almost runs into Stacy, not realizing she has stopped.

Stacy turns to the teen and smiles. "We're here," she says.

The nurse knocks on a nondescript door across the hall from the media room. Zoe nervously gulps, and her posture uncomfortably tightens as they wait for someone to let her in.

As the door opens, Stacy quickly lectures her. "Be nice, be honest, and most important, relax."

To compensate for her nerves, Zoe makes light of the situation by gaping her mouth in a look of shock. "Don't I always?" she asks.

The door flings open before Stacy can answer her sarcastic remark.

A forty-five-year-old woman with a dark slicked-back bun and pinstriped skirt suit greets them with a smile. Her high-heeled black pumps set her several inches taller than Zoe and Stacy. "Hello there, I'm Dr. M," she states.

Her confident demeanor throws Zoe off. Not knowing how to react, she stands speechless, staring at the intimidating woman.

The nurse gives her a slight nudge forward to jolt her from her stupor. "She's all yours! I'll leave you to it," she says.

Zoe tentatively enters the room. She's over-whelmed, jumping at the sound of the door shutting behind her as Stacy exits. The therapy space is straightforward in design. There are only two pieces of furniture in the room: a desk and a sofa. Both are relatively worn, with marks of wear and tear from years of being subjected to patients' painful memories. A file folder, a college-ruled yellow paper notepad, and a black ballpoint pen lie waiting on the surface of the blond oak desk, which is marred with divots and pen marks from fervent note-taking. The only wall decorations are a standard white circular clock and a motivational poster with two monkeys.

The therapist points to an eighties-style broken-in denim loveseat. Having not seen an actual couch since her intake two months prior, Zoe gallops across the room and takes a seat. After sinking into the comfy cushions, she squirms in their softness and sprawls across the faded blue surface. Resting her head against the armrest, she laughs. "Wow, Doc. If I'd known there was a comfy couch like this here, I would have begged to go to therapy last month," she says.

Not replying, the therapist sits at her desk and reviews Zoe's file while her new patient acclimates.

Zoe stretches her arms and places her hands behind her head, aligning her eyes with the inspirational poster on the opposite wall.

The poster exhibits two monkeys dangling from tree branches; the caption below the illustration says, "Hang in there. We all go a little bananas sometimes."

The room's silence, paired with the sound of the therapist jotting notes and the clocks ticking, makes her anxious. Trying to compensate, she attempts to make small talk. Zoe removes a hand from behind her head and points to the poster. "Does that actually motivate people?" she asks. After pausing for a moment, she continues. "Personally speaking, I'm afraid of monkeys." She fills the space in front of her by wiggling the fingers of her hand for a demonstration. "It's the teeny tiny hands... They creep me out."

Dr. M refrains from looking up and continues scribbling notes on her pad.

The silence gets to Zoe, and she sits up from her slouched position and scoots forward to get a better view of what she's writing. Realizing she's too far away to read the small print, she passively tries to get her to share the pages' contents. "Wouldn't it be funny if all you were doing was doodling?" she asks. Her fingers pull the sweater away from her neck so she can get some air, and she awkwardly laughs.

After finishing putting some last thoughts on the paper, the therapist calmly raises her eyes from the notepad to begin the session. "As you already know, my name is Dr. M. I'll be your therapist for the rest of your time here," she says. She smiles warmly. "Let's start by collecting some basic details."

Her hypnotic essence makes Zoe feel a bit more at ease, and she decides to go along with the experience and give the doctor a chance. "All right, shoot. Let's hear what you got," she says.

The therapist stares back down at her notepad and begins writing as she asks her first question. "Your first name is Zoe, correct?"

Zoe quickly nods. "Yup sure is."

Dr. M continues, writing in unison with Zoe's responses. "Your file says you're seventeen years old?"

Zoe smirks. "Well, I just turned seventeen a few days ago. I'm young, dumb, and having fun," she replies. Not receiving a laugh, she chuckles at her own joke. "I mean, aren't your teen years supposed to be the time for trial and error?"

The therapist doesn't react to her justification as she jots down a few more notes. Cutting to the chase, she jumps to the hard questions. "What's your home life like?" she asks.

Her energy shifts as she considers how to answer. The tone of her voice reflects her uncomfortable sentiment surrounding the question as she blurts a response. "Well, it's just my dad and me," she says. Taking a moment of pause, she realizes that was the first time those words had left her lips. Admitting they were the only two at home prompted the memory of her mother's passing to return to the forefront of her mind, and she spins her narrative into a joke to hide her pain. "I tried to get the stork to take me back, but he said I was too heavy," she says with a chuckle.

The therapist pauses her writing and directs her attention to Zoe. "Losing a mother can be tremendously traumatic, especially for a young person," she says. Shifting her concerning tone, she focuses on digging deeper. "How old were you when she passed away?"

As the therapist calmly waits for her reply, the look of pity makes her squirm in her seat. She attempts to distract her mind by picking at a loose thread on the couch. Preferring to not focus on the tragedy, she shrugs and gives a nervous response. "I was eleven, almost twelve. It was like a few years ago. Well, five to be exact."

Dr. M continues to write detailed notes in the file. "When a loved one passes, individuals can compartmentalize the loss, and the buried pain can express itself both inside and out." She takes a deep breath and tries to instill a sense of calm in the room before continuing. "Zoe, would you say the substance abuse started around the time of her passing?"

Not wanting to delve into the details, she anxiously shifts her attention to the monkey poster, hoping to ease her uncomfortable feelings. Finding no relief at the sight of it, she nervously rubs her right wrist and tightly closes her eyes. She winces as she recalls the painful memories, she has worked so hard to bury. While she refrains from making eye contact, her spastic mannerisms shift into embarrassment as she lowers her voice to answer the question. "Sometimes she'd give me some pills out of her stash to calm me down." Her legs nervously twitch, and she pulls them onto the couch, tucking them underneath her to stop their jiggling movement. "Then it escalated after she, you know, was gone." After realizing the information she shared may paint her mother in a poor light, she quickly backtracks, fumbling for words to redeem her character. "It's not like she forced anything on me. She was cool. Everyone loved her. I mean, I loved her." She frantically picks at her nails and locks eyes with the floor.

The therapist continues to take notes and dig for more information. "Have you had a support system during your rehabilitation journey? I was told they gave you phone privileges. Who do you usually call?"

Something is bothering Zoe. She stretches her neck to release some tension and anxiously puts her legs back on the floor to answer. "I was talking to my friend Britt almost weekly, but she must have blocked me. I don't know. She just stopped answering my calls," she says.

Dr. M's eyes lift from the page to observe Zoe's nervous tics. "Did you abuse substances together?" she asks.

Snickering at the formality of her words, Zoe carelessly shrugs. "I mean, I'm in rehab, aren't I? It wasn't always about getting high together all the time... We went through a ton of shit together. We kind of became each other's support systems." The sound of the ticking wall clock distracts her, and as she glances at its face, it stirs a vivid memory of their friendship. Slowly her mind drifts off to when she and Britt indeed became inseparable.

»———«

They met at school in the late spring of 2012, two years after Zoe lost her mother. The two immediately clicked. Britt was the only one who treated Zoe with any sense of normalcy after her mother's death. One Friday night, they decide to have a sleepover. At the time, both girls were barely fourteen. Britt convinced her to skip the last class of the day to go shopping. Wanting to shake the unforgettable memory of her mother's passing from her mind, she agreed to the whim. Since neither was old enough to drive, they walked to the closest store—a supermarket.

A similar clock to the one in the therapy room counted the minutes above the beauty aisle. After playfully skipping down the row of products, they landed in front of the small section containing hair dye.

Britt scanned through every fun color and held them up to Zoe's hair to see how it would look. "Ugh! I hate that you can pull off like every shade," she said.

She grabbed a box containing a crazy neon green color and held it next to Zoe's cheek. After making a funny face to lighten the mood, she placed it back on the shelf. Britt noticed a color swatch of highlighter red hanging nearby and reached for it. "What about this one?" she asked, squinting to pretend she was trying to analyze the compatibility.

Zoe grabbed it from her and raced to the small mirror stuck to the shelving to search for herself. She smiled. " I saw an old picture of my mom with some dope red streaks, so I feel like if she can rock it, by default that means it has to look good on me too. Isn't that how it works? Isn't it like a genetic thing?" Making cute faces in the mirror, she fantasized about her new appearance.

Annoyed by her excitement, Britt lunged forward and snatched it out of her hands. Stepping in front of her, she held the color swatch next to her skin and compared it to herself. "I guess it's kind of like a tribute to her, so I'm into the cute idea," she said with a shrug. After locating the corresponding box of dye, she placed it under her arm and continued to peruse the aisle. Britt stopped at a package of blond hair color and picked it up to view the model's picture on the front of the box. "You know, I've always wondered what it would be like to have some blond streaks." Her ego grew as she struck a pose like the model on the box. "If she can pull it off, I feel like I can too."

Zoe nodded in agreement. "It'll be a fresh start for us," she said.

Holding both cartons of dye, one in each hand, Britt excitedly clapped them together. "Bitch, you're so right," she stated.

Worried her friend's excitement would draw attention to them, she made a hushing sound to get her to quiet. "Were doing this at your house, right?" Zoe asked.

Staring at the boxes in her hands, she hesitated. "Yeah, so about that... My old man's new girlfriend is supposedly staying over tonight, so my place may be a no-go," she said.

The news brought a defeated expression to Zoe's face. Still set on dying her hair red, she quickly conjured up a new plan. "Shit, well, we definitely can't go to my place... My dad has been going off the deep end lately, and when I left for school this morning, it seemed like it might be one of 'those' days... He was already getting angry at the TV for literally not responding to his questions," she said, her arms crossing to cover up her embarrassment over the disclosure.

Britt laughed in disbelief. *The laughter helped Zoe overcome her worry, and she joined in to commiserate over the ridiculousness of the situation.*

Suddenly Britt came up with a brilliant idea. Before speaking, she scanned around them to see if anyone was watching. A sheepish grin came over her lips, and her voice dropped to a whisper. "There's another option... We could do it here." She used the box in her hand to point to the bathroom at the end of the aisle. "Not to mention we probably wouldn't even have to pay for these, so it seems like a win-win."

As the words sank in, the escalating adrenaline of the situation excited her. Zoe scanned the packages of dye, then glanced at the bathroom door and grinned. "I like the way you think."

Her friend's agreement put a massive smile on her face. "Wait, so you are down?" Britt asked.

Zoe shrugged and nodded. "Yeah, fuck it. Let's do it," she said.

They began the momentous occasion with a high five then Britt took off running down the aisle, and Zoe followed. After making their way into the bathroom, they closed the door and assessed their makeshift hair salon.

The restroom had two sparkling-clean white porcelain sinks stationed under a large rectangular mirror, a white-and-gray speckled vinyl floor, white walls, and two separate light-gray stalls. Each girl took her place in front of a sink and opened their respective color selection. When they glanced at their packages, they realized they'd have forgotten they needed mixing bowls. Scanning the room, their eyes simultaneously land back on the two sinks. After securing the sink stoppers, they pulled on the gloves provided in the boxes and squeezed the tubes of dye and developer into the basins. Red in one and blond in the other. They tucked paper towels around their necks and mixed the sinks' contents with their gloved hands. Forgoing the provided brushes, they used their hands as applicators. Britt stuck with straight blond, while Zoe used both colors to create streaks. After rinsing their vinyl-clad fingers, they pulled on the provided caps. The bathroom was a disaster. Dye and empty packaging littered the sinks, counter, and floor. Ignoring the mess, the girls hid in separate bathroom stalls while their hair color finished processing. Becoming impatient, Zoe tapped her feet as she sat on the toilet seat. "How long is this supposed to take? My head itches," she griped.

Britt rolled her eyes at her friend's complaints. She then used her cell phone to search social media posts and DIY hair tutorials. "IDK. The directions said twenty minutes, or maybe it was thirty.:

Britt's lack of a solid time frame made Zoe nervously pick her nails. "You're sure adding the blond will look good with the red?" she asked.

"Of course. Otherwise, I wouldn't have told you to do it!" she exclaimed. "Oh, my God, yes, girl! You seriously need to live a little." Rummaging through her school bag, she pulled out a prescription bottle and vape pen. Her fingers grabbed two pills, which she passed underneath the stall divider to Zoe. "Take this. It'll take the edge off things because you're seriously killing the mood."

Following her direction, Zoe grabbed the pills, placed them on her tongue, and swallowed them. Britt then passed the vape underneath the stall, and Zoe grabbed it.

"I swear that'll be the best cocktail you'll ever have in your life... At least that's what my mom used to say," Britt said with a giggle. Before she took a puff of the vape, she paused. "Wait, I never asked you... What happened to your mom?"

"It was super similar to your situation. She passed away," Britt stated.

"I'm sorry," Zoe said as she deeply inhaled through the vape. The contents made the whites of her eyes turn pink, and her demeanor mellow. She handed the device back under the stall.

Britt took a hit and put the pen back in her bag. "Feeling better?" she asked.

Though Zoe remained still, she felt everything swaying around her. "Much," she said.

As they sat silently, Britt got carried away scrolling through her phone. As she lifted her thumb to tap a photo, she noticed the time and panicked. She hopped to her feet and frantically knocked on the adjoining wall. "Shit, girl, we gotta wash this shit out, like pronto," she said. Quickly, she exited her stall to retrieve her friend and found her slumped against the toilet paper dispenser with her eyes barely open. She tried to pull her up.

Zoe laughed at her attempt. "I can't feel my legs," she said.

After several attempts, Britt got her to her feet, guided her staggering body to the sink, and leaned her over the porcelain bowl. Wasting no time, she turned the faucet on high; Zoe laughed hysterically as water trickled through her hair and down her cheeks. Suddenly Britt felt a bit off, and a sinking feeling set in. Reaching into her pocket, she pulled out her vape and checked the cylinder. Her eyes widened as she realized she had accidentally inserted the high-potency cartridge. "Fuck!"

Britt knew they didn't have long before complete incoherence. Her higher tolerance to substances is their only hope for saving their hair from a dye catastrophe. She grabbed Zoe by the back of the head and dunked her under the water to wash the product out. "We gotta hurry before my high kicks in," she said. Color ran everywhere, and trying to make haste, she left Zoe to wash out her hair in the adjacent sink.

Zoe laughed as she lifted her head from the basin and the extra red colorant ran from her hair down her face. The pigment stained her skin and clothing bright crimson, making it appear as if she were a victim of a massacre. She was too high to stand, her body slumping to the floor and falling against the wall.

Not paying attention to her friend, Britt used the soap from the dispenser to rinse the excess blond from her hair.

A look of horror fell over Zoe's face, and her eyes widened at seeing her clothes drenched in red. "Am I dead?" she asked. Panic ensuing, she frantically pawed at the red stains, convinced it was blood.

Britt pulled her head from under the faucet to investigate the cause of the commotion. As she glimpsed her finished hair in the mirror, she was horrified. Rather than perfect streaks of blond, it's blotchy, with bleached clumps. "I'm ugly!" she cried. As her hands shook, the rest of the narcotic combination set in. Slowly she turned to look at her friend, who was still hysterically crying on the floor, and thinking she was on the verge of death, crawled to be with her in her time of need. "It's all my fault! You died because of me," she said, grabbing Zoe's arm.

Hunched over her knees in a tight ball, Zoe rocks back and forth. "There's blood everywhere! Holy shit! Holy shit! Holy shit!" she said, her red hair sticking to her face.

They both had different lamentable experiences in the same space, less than a foot apart.

Britt panicked. "I'm so ugly. My life is over. Oh, my God, my life is over," she cried.

Shifting from her collapsed position, Zoe wailed as she tilted her head to glare at Britt. "Your life is over? I'm already fucking dead!" she snapped. Her tears became tinted a shade of pink as they rolled down her cheeks. A heavy trash can stood close by, and she reached for it. Using all her strength and mental willpower to convince herself her legs still worked, she pulled herself to her feet. As she held on to the rim, she peered in the large mirror, and the reflection made her howl in horror.

Britt tried to redeem herself by coming to the rescue. Bracing her hand against the wall, she stood and slowly made her way to Zoe. The image of her friend's reflection in the mirror made her pause and turned her skin stark white; it was as if she had seen a ghost. She closed her eyes and tried to focus while reaching out to touch her face. Her eyes sprang open when her fingers contacted her skin, and her pupils dilated with paranoia. "Why can I feel your face? Does that mean I'm dead too?" Britt asked. Her fingers retracted to her sides as fear ran through her veins.

They fell silent at the epiphany as they stared at each other. Slowly they turned in unison toward the mirror, and their mouths gaped open, releasing glass-shattering screams.

The bathroom door abruptly opened, and a female employee rushed inside to investigate the racket. Her face donned heavy makeup to hide her age. She was holding a mop and was dressed in a light-gray embroidered polo, faded blue jeans that were too small, and a navy-blue regulation apron with an embroidered smiley face sun. Above her right breast was a name tag that read, "Marge." Each brown strand of hair in her messy updo is frizzy from having cleaned the bathroom earlier that day. As she lowered her wood-and-yarn weapon, she scanned the atrocious mess the girls made.

Frozen like zombies, they stared at the woman in the mirror's reflection. They believe that if they stay still, she won't see them.

The woman slowly backs away in disbelief. "I'm not paid enough for this," she said, shaking her head as she rushed out to call the cops.

The girls' high escalated as they meandered to the store's exit. The next thing they knew, they were blind-

ed by the lights of a police car flashing at them through its backseat window. To make matters worse, the reflection of a displeased officer's face glared at them from the rearview mirror. Glancing at each other, they smirked and laughed.

⇥ ·•· ⇤

The sound of the ticking clock on the wall ends her daydream.

Emotional happiness lingers from the fun memory of her best friend, and she warmly smiles at the brief thought. Reorienting herself, she turns her attention back to Dr. M. "Uh, sorry, what was the question?" she asks.

The therapist clears her throat, then says, "Did your friend abuse substances with you, and if so, was it often?"

Thinking back to the flashback, Zoe uncomfortably pauses and nods. "Yeah, she did, and I guess you could call it often," she says, looking at the clock. She continues to listen for the sound of each tick, hoping it will lull her into another daydream about her friend.

The therapist finishes writing her notes, and her lips purse as she sets her pen down to speak. "Often, during your road to sobriety, those who enabled your addiction may push you away, and that's okay. It may seem difficult now, but our mission is to get you healthy."

Shifting her gaze, Zoe makes eye contact and nods, accepting the harsh reality. "Yeah, I know." She glances at the floor to mask her sadness while trying to find the silver lining. "You know, my uncle has been pretty supportive through this thing; he's like my redo dad," she says.

Dr. M picks up the pen to jot down a few more notes. "That's wonderful. How's your relationship with your father?" she asks.

The inquisition triggers memories that spark Zoe's anger, causing her fists to clench. Never having been given the opportunity to genuinely express her opinions about him, every word spews out her mouth like a tsunami. "He's a drunken asshole who only got worse when my mom died. Luckily for him, I got pretty good at covering that shit up during home visits." Her breathing quickens.

The therapist sets down her pen, gets up from behind her desk, and moves across the room to sit next to Zoe on the couch.

She tries to comfort her, but Zoe pulls away. "This shit is embarrassing," she states.

Dr. M's lips form a warm smile to reassure her. "Nothing is embarrassing; always remember that. We can only get better by mending all facets of life, especially what's buried inside."

Zoe looks at the doctor and, feeling safe, gives a small smile back.

As they share a moment of understanding, the therapist looks into her eyes to drive her point home. "You are important, and you are worth it," she states.

While they briefly sit in silence, Zoe wipes a tiny tear from the corner of her eye.

The therapist leisurely gets up from the worn sofa and steps toward the exit. She then turns to look at Zoe. "You made amazing progress today. How do you feel?"

Enjoying her last minutes on the comfortable couch, she sniffles and shrugs. "Good, I guess," she says, then gets up and follows the therapist to the door.

Sensing a breakthrough, Dr. M lightly places a hand on her patient's shoulder. "We're all proud of you, Zoe. You're doing extremely well on your road to recovery,"

The door slowly opens, breaking up their moment, and they both turn to see who is entering.

Stacy pokes her head inside and grins. "We're all proud of you," she says.

Never having felt this much support before, she flashes them a genuine grin of happiness. To her, they're catalysts for her internal change.

Chapter Ten

HOME SWEET HOME

After that pivotal moment, an entire month passes without Zoe realizing it. She has found the staff to be the family she never had. Her existence becomes easier each day of her stay, and her new routine is comforting. Zoe climbs out of bed with the rising sun and puts on her real-world clothes: an old vintage shirt, baggy ripped jeans, and checkered slip-on shoes. She exercises her steady breathing while listening to the chirping birds outside the window. "You'll be fine. You got this," she states as she walks toward an empty cardboard box Stacy left on her desk. She slowly packs her things, remembering the good and bad times she's had during her stay. With her entire box of memories in hand, she walks over, sits on the edge of the bed, and stares at the whiteboard.

The board is back to her prearrival state; any evidence of her treatment plan and diagnosis has been erased, signifying her fresh start.

Although Zoe has pictured this day for a long while, she's anxious, not knowing how to process the fact that it has arrived. As she overthinks what life will be like outside the walls where she finds endless support, the door crashes open, and she snaps her head to look.

Stacy barges in wearing a giant smile and rushes across the room to give her an enormous hug. "Today's the big day!" she says.

Still feeling her nerves creeping up, Zoe forces herself to stand. Knowing she should be happy, she tentatively grins. Her lips quiver as she recip-rocates the hug.

Stacy rubs Zoe's back. "Congrats on your sobri-ety. We're all so proud of you." Releasing her from the embrace, she takes a moment to analyze the teen's face. "How are you feeling? Did you gather all your things?" she asks.

Trying to play it cool, Zoe turns to reach for her box of belongings on the bed and takes a deep breath. "It's crazy—I feel like I have a new lease on life," she says. She redirects her thoughts by laughing as her eyes well with tears. "My only concern is I might not remember how to do my makeup," she adds with a smirk.

The nurse joins her in laughter and crosses her arms. Shrugging, she grins. "I have to say I'll miss your sarcasm."

Hiding her emotions, Zoe nervously tightens her grip around the cardboard as her feet walk for the door.

Feeding into the presumption that Zoe is excited to be free, Stacy remains upbeat, giggling as she exuberantly shares information from the other side of the room. "Oh, before I forget, your uncle parked your car outside. He couldn't get off his shift and left the keys in the ignition so you'd have a way to get home. He wanted to make sure you were good."

Zoe shifts the box to rest on her hipbone. Turning around, she chuckles sarcastically. "Oh, goodie! At least I have one decent family member." She masks her welling tears with a huge smile and dramatically winks. "I hope I never see you again, Stacy." Not able to bear seeing her response, she turns to face the door.

Reciprocating, Stacy dishes back the sarcasm. "I hope I never see you again too," she says. As she watches her exit, she remembers one more thing. "By the way, I left a little present on your car key ring to remember us!"

Zoe throws up a peace sign with her free hand to thank her. Wanting to avoid the possibility of any further conversation, she re-grips the box and races through the hall toward the front exit.

Escaping the building's heavy glass doors, she smells freedom as the sun's rays hit her skin. Having no way to shield her eyes from the glare, she sprints across the hot asphalt in search of her car's refuge. Standing in the center of a large lot of vehicles, she spins in a quick circle to scan the lot. Relief rushes over her as she spots a beat-up pale-yellow Volkswagen convertible. "Good ol' faithful," she says with a smile.

The car's dirty cream-colored soft top, a multi-tude of minor scuffs and scratches, and a vanity plate that reads, "Zoe", give the vehicle character.

The day is unusually warm, and wanting to escape the heat, she quickly opens the car door and climbs inside. She settles her body onto the scratched leather driver's-side seat and turns around, tossing her small box of belongings to the bench seat in the back. The sun's scorching rays beating down on the idle car have made the interior oven-like, and smell of crayons. The familiarity of the childhood odor oddly comforts her as her hands rest on the wheel. She takes a moment to admire the pair of fuzzy dice and a butterfly decoration hanging from her rearview mirror. Even though she knows it'll be hot to the touch, her hand rubs the black dashboard. "Missed you, gal," she says. Reaching for the keys in the ignition, she notices the gift Stacy referred to.

The collection of keyring bobbles freely hangs, showcasing her familiar panda-themed lanyard, fuzzy yellow puffball, sparkly letter Z, and now a Narcotics Anonymous keychain to signify her accomplishment of becoming sober.

Her fingertips move to touch the fresh addition, and she rubs the metal charm with a grin. As she turns the key to start the engine, she looks over the hood and smirks after catching sight of the pair of black plastic eyelashes she glued above the head-lights before entering rehab. The revving engine fills her with excitement. She pushes the convert-ible button above the sticker-adorned rearview mirror and retracts the top to enjoy the beautiful weather. Sunshine pours into her topless car as she opens the glove compartment to find a pair of sunglasses. The large frames contain translucent lenses the color of a tequila sunrise; putting them on makes her reminisce about the taste of alcohol. Fighting the urge, she inhales a deep breath of air and turns on the radio to help divert her attention.

Pulling out of the parking lot feels like the most significant accomplishment of her life. She navi-gates the urban streets leading to the freeway and down a country road. Even though her drive only takes thirty minutes, knowing what's on the other side of her journey makes it feel like a lifetime.

She puts on her blinker to turn down a side road and reads the sign marking the street aloud: "Polk

Road." The familiarity of the Podunk neighborhood makes her heart race. As her tires transition from pavement to gravel, her hands tremble uncontrollably, and she slows her speed.

Peering from a distance, at the end of the cul-de-sac of misfits, is her childhood home.

Her right-hand lifts from the steering wheel to turn the music down and lower the sunglasses to the bridge of her nose so she can get a more detailed look. "Home sweet home," she mutters. As she gets closer, she sees the unkempt yard and the rusted metal of the swing set outside the small dwelling. "I can't believe I grew up in this dump." Uncertain of what she'll encounter and hoping to enter unnoticed, she pulls her car up to the curb and parks in front of the neighbor's house. Immediately she turns off the vehicle and, for extra precaution, leaves the key in the ignition to prepare for a swift departure. Upon exiting the car, she quietly shuts the door and freezes at the sight of where she grew up.

The single-wide trailer with chipped oxidized white paint sits on a cinder block foundation in the middle of an overgrown lot. A rusty double-size swing set stands abandoned in the center of a cluster of weeds. The breeze moves the sun-damaged dark-blue plastic seats. With each sway, harsh screeches penetrate Zoe's ears, the childhood sound triggering feelings of unease to fill her gut.

Closing her eyelids, she clenches her jaw and whispers under her breath to convince her feet to move. "It's like a Band-Aid. You just got to rip it off and get it over with," she states. Her eyes open, and she compulsively picks at her nails. Knowing she must gather some of her belongings before leaving for good, she reluctantly forces herself to walk toward the front door. As she makes her way down the makeshift path, the sight of the swings and the distinct smell of the blooming ragweed forces her mind into a flashback of her childhood.

⇥ ⋅⧓⋅ ⇤

The yard's layout was identical but a bit better maintained, and the swing set's metal was shiny green with very little rust.

Her six-year-old self joyously pumped her legs to go higher with each back-and-forth swing, her innocent giggles filling the air. Even though her overalls were dirty and her hair appeared to have been unbrushed for days, she was content.

Fresh into his thirties, her father watched her play-ing from a blue-and-white-striped jelly lawn chair. His light facial scruff was unkempt, and his untrimmed, greasy hair messily hung over his ears and past his brows. Matching his daughter's disheveled appear-ance, he wore a yellow-stained wife beater, a torn blue flannel shirt, and baggy jean shorts that sagged, ex-posing the top of his faded boxer briefs. Five crushed beer cans surrounded his dirty bare feet and the met-al legs of his fold-out chair. Reaching into the small blue cooler beside him, he grabbed and opened a fresh cold one. Smiling, he shouted across the lawn to his daughter. "I told you Daddy would take care of you!" Taking a moment to belch, he continued. "Didn't I?"

The wind tousling Zoe's hair made her grin wildly.

Her laughter caused him to smile as he took another sip. "It's just you and me, bud." He chugged the rest of the can and crushed it with one hand. "Always remember that." Wasting no time, he grabbed an-

other brew. As he took his first sip, the sound of an approaching car distracted him.

A nineties BMW with oxidized black paint, keyed scratch marks, and black-tinted windows pulled into the driveway and screeched to a stop. The engine continued to run as the vehicle idled next to the yard.

Zoe's dad didn't recognize the car. With a beer in hand, he got up to take a closer look. The bright sun made him squint, and he used his hand to shade his eyes while glaring at the dark windows. The passenger door swung open.

A woman in her early twenties stumbled out of the car and shut the door. Her eyes were surrounded by day-old smeared smoky eyeliner, and her ombre hair with red-streaked accents appeared slept on. It was Zoe's mother. After barely making her way to the yard, she pulled down on her ripped denim Minnie skirt, which rode up her fishnet stockings.

As the little girl spotted her mother mid-swing, her eyes lit up with a toothy smile. "Mommy!" she exclaimed.

Taking another sip of his beer, Zoe's dad remained standing in his place.

Still intoxicated, Zoe's mother tripped on her denim-colored wedges, tumbling to the ground as she stepped from the pavement onto the soft grass. Her ride quickly backed up and sped off as she lay on her back, laughing. Shifting her weight, she rolled over to her belly and stared up at her swinging daughter. "Hi, baby girl!" she said, wiggling over to her hands and knees to haphazardly stand.

The little girl's father glared at his wife as she weaved her way to the swing set. As resentment built in his eyes, he chugged his can of brew to cope.

Not bothering to acknowledge him, Zoe's mom passed by without a word, speaking only to her daughter. "Have you gotten bigger?" she asked; her hand motioned for her to approach, as though she were calling a dog. "Come down here and see your mama," she slurred.

Zoe's father can't take standing by any longer. After tossing his empty can to the ground, he rushed to stand between them. Facing his unmanageable wife, he threw his hands in the air. "Where the fuck have you been?" he snarled.

His intensity made her laugh, and she fell back to the ground. "What are you...my dad? Why the fuck do you even care?" she asked.

Moving closer, he glared down at her with a red face and clenched fists. After taking a moment to paste on a passive-aggressive smile, he turned to address the playing child. "Sweetie, you remember that game we like to play that's like an Easter egg hunt, but better?" he asked.

Still swinging, Zoe smiled while bobbing her head with an enthusiastic nod.

He slowed the pace of his speech to make it easier for her to understand. "Mommy doesn't feel well, so I'm going to take her inside so she can nap. Now close your eyes, cover your ears, and count to one hundred real slow. Promise me you'll keep playing until I get back and no peeking."

Zoe was beside herself that someone wanted to play with her, so she immediately stopped swinging to close her eyes tightly. "All right, Daddy. I promise!" she exclaimed. Her fingers plugged her ears as her tiny voice shouted the first number.

As he turned back to glare at his wife sprawled on the ground, his festering anger triggered a crazed look in his eyes.

His wife had seen that look many times before, but rather than cower, she sneered at him. "What are you going to do? Huh? Is the big man going to hit me?" she asked. His lack of response made her laugh, and she pointed to her cheek. "Try me. I got enough Xanax in me to be your fucking punching bag for days. I promise you I won't feel a thing."

Enraged by her words, he lunged forward and grabbed a handful of her long wavy hair. "Shut your fucking mouth!" he barked. With a jerking motion, he dragged her to her feet. "If I knew you were such a slut, I never would have touched your filthy ass and knocked you up."

As vile insults were common between them, she was untroubled by the interaction. Rather than back away, she mocked him with sarcasm and laughter. "Well, since I fucked you, wouldn't that make us both sluts?" In anger, she lifted her finger and pointed to the compliantly counting child. "Only mistake I made was keeping that little bitch."

Filled with rage, he tightened his grip on her hair and struck her. The act filled him with a sense of control and satisfaction. Grabbing a more significant fistful of her red-streaked locks, his clenched fingers dragged her petite unconscious frame into the house. After tossing her inside, he peered out to confirm the child was still counting and slammed the door behind them.

"One hundred!" young Zoe said, opening her eyes. After hopping off the swing, she skipped around the yard, picking up the crushed beer cans littering the lawn. As her naïve giggles filled the air, screams emanated from the home's four walls.

⊷•◦•⊶

The memory is vivid, to the point that she can hear her younger self's laughter lingering in the distance. Thinking about the past causes her jaw to tighten. Before she can second-guess her decision to collect her things, her feet make their way to the trailer's front door. Zoe avoids eye contact with the swing set as she passes it. She pauses, inches away from the faux wood entry, and her heart races.

Even though there's no car in the driveway, she's unsure if her father is home. Because of his drinking problem, he has racked up many DUIs, causing the state to seize his car on multiple occasions. Her fingers uncontrollably shake as she quietly twists the knob. When she peeks in to scan her surroundings, she's met with her worst fear. The sound of the TV draws her attention to the recliner, and she notices her dad's passed-out body.

His nostrils produce a loud snore as he lies sprawled on the stained light-brown corduroy recliner. Crushed beer cans and remnants of potato chips are scattered across the shag rug. He's wearing the same outfit she recounted from her memory of the yard scene, and the sight terrifies her.

As she tiptoes across the floor to her room while holding her breath, Zoe hopes her father only recently passed out. Upon reaching her bedroom door, she releases a deep exhalation. Just as she feels safe, she hears a floorboard creak behind her, and her entire body trembles with fear.

The sway of her father's heavy limbs makes the floorboard creak again. As he clears his throat, he slurs his words. "Where the fuck have you been?"

She reluctantly turns toward the sound of his voice.

Raising his fist, he hits the wall in the hallway lined with old family photos. The impact causes pictures to crash to the floor and creates a hole in the drywall. Glass shatters around their feet.

The noise of the destruction makes her wince, then stand paralyzed with anxiety. She tries to speak but loses her last bit of courage as she looks down and notices a large cut on her father's fist caused by the broken glass. As blood drips to the floor, she desperately grasps for a single word.

He takes a staggering step and yells. "Goddamn it, answer me!"

She tries to comply, but nothing comes out.

Stumbling closer, he continues to harass her. "Where the fuck have you been?" he asks as she takes a small step back. "Huh? Have you been fucking the neighbors again?" he shouts as he stabilizes his wavering body against the wall. Looking to the ground, he incoherently mumbles. "Why don't you do it already? Just leave Zoe and me. Our lives would be better without you anyway."

Upon processing his words, she realizes he believes she is her mother. Thinking she can defuse the situation, she slowly steps toward him. "Dad, it's me. I'm Zoe." Her body leans closer, and her trembling voice softens. " Mom is dead..." Before she can finish, he bashes her rib cage in a fit of rage, knocking her to the floor.

His momentum causes his staggering feet to lose balance, and he falls after her.

Her eyes grow wide as she watches him lying unconscious on the floor beside her, his eyes half-open. As she tries to catch her breath, she notices one of the broken frames next to his head. It holds a picture of the three of them together from when she was a toddler; the sight causes all her pent-up memories of abuse to flood back. The correlation triggered PTSD she didn't even realize she carried with her. Stunned by what just happened, she tries to calm down by curling into a fetal position. Her body goes numb as she tries to detach herself from the situation. She feels like she's stuck in her horrific childhood all over again.

Thinking her father is dead, she slowly crawls to check his pulse, but before she can touch him, his mouth opens.

He rolls back and forth as if tossing and turning from a bad dream. "I never should have married a whore. You made me this way. This is all your fault," he says. As his speech trails off, he begins to snore.

Seeing her opportunity to escape, Zoe crawls to the bathroom to grab her things. Reaching the sink, she grasps the edge of the countertop to stabilize herself. Her wobbly knees feel like unsettled jelly as she stands. Slowly her shaking hands lift to wipe the tears away from her puffy eyes. To distract herself, she rummages through the cabinet for eyeliner to make herself feel prettier. She finds her mother's old blue faux fur-trimmed cosmetic bag still packed with her personal items and sets it on the counter. The sight of her belongings brings her comfort, as though her mother is present and watching over her. After unzipping the bag, she retrieves a half-used black eyeliner pencil and frantically applies it. She opens the drawers and, after finding all her stuff, adds it to the open cosmetic pouch.

Quietly, she pokes her head outside the door to make sure her dad is still motionless before running down the short hallway to her bedroom to grab some clothes. Once in her room, she shuts and locks the door behind her. Pressing her back against the wall, she sinks to the floor—her world is unraveling around her. She clutches her hair and focuses on breathing as she rocks back and forth to prevent a panic attack. After a few moments, she regains her composure. Reality sets in, and she knows she doesn't have long. "I have to get the fuck out of here," she says, standing up.

She races to her closet to fetch an old yellow canvas backpack and a forest-green duffel. After packing her mom's vanity bag, she grabs whatever clothes are in sight, then crams them into the green nylon satchel. "Where am I going to go? Come on, Zoe, think." She runs to her dresser to grab more stuff. Tapping her head, she scans her room one last time to make sure she has every-thing. "Adam? What about him?" Her feet sprint to grab her collected possessions, and she searches her yellow school backpack to see what she left inside. "I'm such a moron—I don't even have a phone!" As she digs through her bag while devising a plan, the pain from her broken rib sets in. She winces." What about Britt?" Her feet pace beneath her. "No. Fuck Britt. She's dead to me... She ditched me while I was in rehab. Who even does that?"

A loud moan echoes from the hallway. It's her father. He's awake.

The sound triggers her to freeze. Filled with sheer panic, she quickly zips her bags. After slinging them over her shoulders, she heads to the window while trying to convince herself that things will be all right. "I have a car; that's all I need. I'll just drive and figure it out. People do it all the time. It'll be like a road trip," she says, sliding the window open. The doorknob violently shakes behind her. She jumps. Scanning her room one last time, she sees a framed family photo taken the week before her mother's passing. She runs, grabs it from the dresser, and pulls it from the frame. After tearing her father out of the picture, she crumples up the torn image of him, tosses it to the floor, and stuffs the rest of the photo inside the yellow canvas. Reclosing her bag, she catches sight of the patch sewn onto the front and rubs it for good luck. "Not dead yet," she says, looking to the open window. Trying to make light of the situation, she shrugs. "Could be worse; at least I'm on the first floor."

The hollow-core door can't protect her from the deafening sound of violent pounding and brutal words.

After sprinting back to the window, she tosses out her belongings and follows closely behind. The moment her feet hit the lawn, she hears the bedroom door being kicked in behind her, and without looking back, she runs as fast as she can to her car.

Her father continues to scream obscenities in the distance.

She chucks her green bag into the backseat and the backpack on the passenger side. Knowing she's almost out of time, she doesn't bother opening the latch and instead hops over the car door. As she takes a deep breath, her jaw clenches at the unbearable pain radiating from her ribs. Her trembling hand starts the ignition, and with her foot heavy on the gas pedal, she peels out, making her getaway. As she looks in the rearview mirror, the view of her childhood home becomes hazy from the dust kicked in the air by her squealing tires. She turns her eyes back to the road as the sight of her terrible memories vanishes in the distance.

 Chapter Eleven

ROAD TRIP

As Zoe drives through the night, her eyes grow tired, and the reflectors on the road blur. Still, she knows she can't stop. Only seventeen and considered a minor in the eyes of the law, she knows it'll only be a matter of time before her dad sobers up enough to file a missing person report on her behalf. With each passing moment, she feels closer to freedom, and the exhilaration causes her foot to press heavier on the gas. She sticks to the highway and counts every new city limit sign she passes. It becomes a thrilling game for her as she lets fate guide her path.

Radio stations change, hours pass, and the scenery shifts. The chilly wind from the retracted convertible top is the only thing keeping her awake. The sight of the rising sun peeking over the desert ridgeline reveals complete desolation. Each minute that passes feels like a century to her weary mind. The sharp pain in her side subsides as she squints to focus on not falling asleep at the wheel.

A hand-painted sign advertises an upcoming gas station.

As Zoe hasn't seen a single sign of life for some time, the cheaply made marker gives her hope that others are nearby. She glances at her dash to see how much gas she has left and notices the marker is just above empty. Since she doesn't know the area or have a map to follow, her mind goes wild with the fear of being stranded. The station approaches, and she makes a last-minute decision to fill the tank. Flipping on her blinker, she doesn't hear the rhythm of the flashing light and loudly sighs after remembering it went out before she was checked into rehab. With no other cars in view, she quickly turns the wheel to pull in.

Desert and tumbleweeds surround the gas station, giving it an eerie backroad ambiance. A small market with an attached tin garage that houses a mechanic shop sits behind a single pumping station. It appears to be nothing more than a converted cattle shed with glass windows.

Zoe slowly pulls her car up to the pump, shifts the gear into park, and turns off the ignition. The fluorescent lights glowing through the store's windows catch her attention. Wanting to ensure she looks presentable after her long dusty drive, she flips the visor down and checks her appearance in the mirror. After noticing dark circles, she angrily flips the plastic rectangle back up to avoid looking at herself. Frustrated with everything and wanting to get back on the road, she rolls her eyes. "I'm so over this right now," she says. After grabbing the gas handle, she checks the price listed on the pump—and it's higher than she expected. Reluctantly she puts the hose back in its holder, and her fingers dig into her scalp to combat her disappointment. "Fuck. Why didn't I think about needing cash?" She sarcastically chuckles and continues to beat herself up verbally. "Some teen runaway. I am... I can't even do that right," she says.

The sun rises higher over the terrain, sending warm rays of light that beat down on the car's interior.

She hunches over the steering wheel to escape the heat while sulking in her misery. As she approaches the height of her self-inflicted criticism, loneliness overcomes her, and Adam pops into her head. "I'm sure, just like everyone else, he's moved on. I know I wouldn't want a broke loser if I were him," she mumbles. Her voice sounds muffled as she talks into the leather wheel. As she replays the morning after their wild night together, the memory of him handing her twenty dollars returns to her.

A murder of crows crowds together in a nearby Joshua tree, watching her as they tauntingly caw.

The hopeful memory of having cash causes her to cut short her pitiful reminiscing. Her head springs from the steering wheel as she tries to remember which outfit she was wearing. Her abrupt movement causes a sharp pain to enter her rib cage, and she moans. Slowly she shallows her breaths to take the edge off the excruciating pain while fighting the urge to give in to the ache. Through her added focus, she finds that her thoughts become more vivid, and the image of the skirt she wore that night flashes back to her. She uses the rearview mirror to look at the luggage in the backseat. "If I was a twenty-dollar bill, where would I be?" she says. Using her right hand to support her side, she fights the pain as she tries to climb over the seat to rummage through her cardboard box of belongings.

It's the first item she encounters on her search and the skirt still has the same dirt stains from the night of the party.

She snatches it up and turns every pocket inside out. As she becomes impatient, she holds the garment up and frantically shakes it. Finally, the infamous bill falls to her lap like a gliding snowflake. She aggressively grabs it and straightens out the crinkles. "Yes!" she exclaims. Excitement builds in her body, and her lips lightly kiss the cash. Amid her glee, she spots the glimmering threads of the good luck patch sewn onto her backpack and rubs it with her pointer finger. She secures the twenty-dollar bill in her bra for safekeeping, and thinking of her near nervous breakdown, she chuckles. "Thank God for Adam," she says. Feeling better about her situation, she hops out of the car and pulls the nozzle from the holster.

As she unscrews the cap on her fuel tank, she notices a man in his early twenties staring at her from the convenience store window. His stick-thin structure and scarred face give away his recreational habit of dabbling with meth. The image of him trying to creep on her in his gray store-issued short-sleeved button-up makes her chuckle. "Do I seem like the type of person who would fill and ditch?" she calls out, smiling and waving at him.

Realizing he's been caught, he hurries away from the glass.

Shaking her head, Zoe secures the nozzle in the car, and as it fills, she reaches into the backseat to grab a change of clothes. Wanting something comfortable, she pulls out a pair of torn denim shorts and a wife beater. After placing them under her arm, she walks toward the market to find the restroom. Not finding an external bathroom, she continues her search inside. As she opens the door to the store, a bell jingles to sound her entrance.

The clerk makes eye contact with her.

Zoe holds the clothes up with a smile. "You got a bathroom I can use?" she asks.

The man points to a stained door next to the refrigerated-beverage section.

Thinking his lack of words is odd, she hustles to the grimy door and retreats inside.

While she changes, the store clerk watches the closed access like a hawk, fantasizing about what she looks like stripping, while rubbing the hard rising bulge in his pants against the low edge of the counter. The sound of the door unlocking ends his daydream, and her exit back into the store causes him to clear his throat.

Knowing the amount of money she has may be short, she purposefully goes bra-less under the thin white material of her tank and nonchalantly makes her way to the counter to pay. She reaches into the pile of her old clothing and pulls out the twenty-dollar bill. As her fingers slide it across the counter, she becomes disgusted by his stare. "What the fuck are you staring at, buddy?" she asks.

The confrontation makes him nervous, and his forehead sweats. He stutters to make a sentence. "Uh...uh... Nothing, ma'am," he says. Forgetting how much to charge her, he quickly shoves the twenty-dollar bill into the cash register and pulls out a five-dollar bill for change. His quivering hand holds out the peace offering.

Staring at him like a zombie, Zoe breaks character to snatch it away and sarcastically smiles. "Thanks!" she states, hustling out of the store. Worried he'll discover the snafu, she sprints across the small parking lot and throws the used clothes in the backseat. Next, she removes the gas nozzle from the car and places it back in the holder to leave. As she races to the driver's seat, she notices the clerk still creepily peering at her through the window, and her body shudders. Wanting to get away as fast as possible, she hops inside and starts the car.

As the engine sounds, the arrow on the gas gauge moves to "full."

She grins. "Life is good," she says, shifting the car into drive. Speeding away, she flips off the gawking clerk and shouts, "Hope you enjoy your boner!" As she laughs at his ridiculous behavior, she cranks up the radio.

After a few hours of driving through the desert, she feels the scenario is mundane. Peering at the clock on the radio, she takes notice of the date.

It reads, "June 10, 2015".

Continuing where she has left off, she checks her appearance in the visor mirror, closes it, and reaches to adjust the rearview mirror to get another angle of her tongue. As she shifts the mirror's position, she uses too much force, and it over-corrects to face the floor. Multitasking to fix her error, she notices the silhouette of a girl walking down the road in the distance, and thinking it might be a mirage, she uses her free hand to rub her eyes. When she takes another glance, the figure is still there, and she squints to get a better view. The notion of someone meandering in the desert makes her chuckle. "What kind of dumbass would hitchhike out here?" Feeling a little lonely from her lengthy drive, she turns down her blasting music to sneak up on the wonder and get a closer look.

As the girl's long loosely curled ombre hair flows in the wind, she dances with each step to techno music she listens to through earbud headphones. Her two-piece denim outfit emulates the uniform

of a galactic warrior princess and perfectly matches her denim-print wedged heels.

Coming to a crawl with her car to match the girl's
speed, Zoe shouts to get her attention. "Hey!" she
says.

The girl hums to the beat of the music she is listening to and is complacent with her surroundings.

As Zoe slowly creeps with her Slug Bug, she yells
louder. "Hey, crazy girl!" she says. Still receiving no
response, she aggressively lays her hand on the
horn.

The jarring sound frightens the girl, who immediately turns around to defend herself and yanks a
single earbud from her ear.

Matching her stop, she notices the teen's profile
looks oddly familiar and hurriedly puts the car into
park. Initially, she can't quite recognize her underneath the heavy make-up, glitter, and jewel forma-
tions around her eyes and red-streaked space-bun
hairdo. "Do I know you from somewhere?" Zoe
says.

Dressed in a skimpy nineties-era metallic accented boho outfit, she shivers from the cold breeze
and pushes back her long dyed red chunks of hair

that hang down like long messy bangs to her jaw-line, unveiling a better view of her features.

They both act like they've seen ghosts as they sit on the side of the desert road staring at each other.

The girl makes the first move to break the silence and rushes to the passenger side. " Zoe? This can't be real... Considering I haven't seen you in months, this must be a sign from the universe." Leaning over the door, she points to her face. "It's me, Britt!" she states.

A dramatic look of shock takes over Zoe's expression, and she doesn't know what to think. Since she didn't know which direction she was driving, the chances of her ending up in the same vicinity as the festival she was invited to blows her mind and leaves her speechless.

Britt interprets her friend's lack of response as rude. "You do remember Adam Schaffer's party, don't you? You know, the last time we hung out before the rehab thing?" she asks. Growing annoyed with her lack of cooperation to converse, she rolls her eyes and playfully puts her weight on the doorframe to relieve her sore feet. "Girl, come on. It hasn't even been that long!" she says.

It is the oddity of the circumstance and buried resentment that drives Zoe's lack of speech, and she slumps in her driver's seat to think.

Britt becomes impatient that her friend has yet to offer her a ride or a place to sit. A minute or so passes as she neurotically continues attempts at motivating an invitation. Lifting her finger, she lightly taps her nose. "I'm always the life of the party, the one who opens the slopes for business, but Dale was being a real asshole that night and held me up with his bullshit," she states, crossing her arms.

The random details snap Zoe from her reflection. There is no question that it is her former best friend underneath the new hairstyle and gaudy festival attire but Zoe is bothered by the harsh reality of being abandoned the night of the party and the events that transpired after. Still hurt, she plays stupid and remains silent to teach her a lesson.

Britt stomps her feet like an angry pony as she throws a fit. She sticks out her tongue and points to it with a high-pitched grunt. "Now let me see yours," she says.

Remaining silent, Zoe gets comfortable in the driver seat's broken leather and holds in her laughter regarding Britt's ridiculous behavior. Keeping her composure, she shakes her head. "No."

The unusual lack of compliance makes Britt panic, and she leans forward and quickly pokes her tongue in and out as an example. "Like this! Please," she begs with a sad puppy-dog look in her eyes.

No longer able to take the endless harassment dealt by her, Zoe breaks her composure and does what she asks. "Like this?" She smirks.

The sight of the infamous tongue ring makes her squeal with excitement. "God, we've had so many good times together!" she states, clapping her hands and jumping up and down.

Nodding in agreement, Zoe places her index fingers on both temples and stares toward the horizon. Pretending to have a psychic vision, she sarcastically snickers as her mind becomes distracted by the memory of the party. "You know what? I think everything is coming back to me now."

Britt is annoyed by the dragging conversation and shifts her body weight to give the blisters on her feet a break. Running out of tactics to hurry up Zoe's invitation to ride along, she leans farther over the car door and wildly waves her hands to pull her out of her daze.

The fanning air wakes Zoe from the pleasant reflection, and she smiles from ear to ear. She shouts to show her excitement. "So fucking epic! That was the night I was pissed at my dad and stole my mom's old bottle of Xanax. I was so shit-faced, I don't remember anything besides that." Thinking of her reckless behavior, she laughs hysterically.

Britt uses the reminiscence of their wild night together as a way to solidify their connection and secure a ride. As she passively chuckles, her hand darts through the air to emphasize her remark. "Well, you got freaky with Adam... Such a little slut," she says.

Her attempt to add ammunition to the fire triggers the memory of Zoe walking home alone after the party and swiftly causes the excitement to dissipate from her face. As her happiness turns to anger, her face tightens with resentment. "Actually...The more I think about it, you left me with no ride, and then you fucking abandoned me in rehab." She closes her eyes to quell her escalating emotions and, taking a gulp, anxiously picks at the goosebumps on her leg. "Also, why did you block me on your phone? I honestly shouldn't even be talking to you right now." To avoid seeing her reaction, she glances down at her backpack resting on the passenger seat.

The unexpected reaction fills Britt with desperation. She pleads with every ounce of manipulative influence as the scuffed soles of her wedges nervously tap the ground. She knows she must make up a narrative for her friend to pity her if she is to get a ride, and running out of options, she'll do whatever it takes. Shifting her tone, her voice cracks to emulate sadness. "Come on, Zoe. Look at me. I had no choice that night. You know how Dale gets, and I swear I didn't even notice I blocked you."

Thoughts of being alone and the justification for her excuses cause Zoe to rationalize her behavior, and she becomes torn about how to react. Finally, her expression softens, and she moves her gaze to analyze Britt's face, searching for any sign that she's being genuine.

They share a moment of silence.

Worried she'll be left alone without anyone who can relate to and understand her side of things, Zoe determines she has no choice but to remedy the relationship. Whether it's good, bad, or neutral, she misses their time together. Taking a deep breath, she embraces her forgiveness and diverts the blame toward the only other individual mentioned. "Fucking Dale." She rolls her eyes to show her disapproval of him. "Are you still together?"

Britt diverts her eyes to the dusty ground to cover her lie and shakes her head no to answer the question.

The response is good enough, and Zoe eases her attitude. "I hate how I can never stay mad at my bestie." She laughs and pats the patch on her backpack to invite her inside. "Don't be a stranger. Climb on in," she states, tossing the bag into the backseat with the rest of her things.

Seizing the opportunity, Britt squeals a thank-you, then flings the door open, hops inside, and stretches out her feet to make herself comfortable.

Before the door is fully closed, Zoe presses on the gas and takes off down the dusty road. The momentum from the car's abrupt acceleration triggers the door to slam shut, and the girls laugh.

With both hands on the wheel, Zoe intently focuses on the road ahead. Her eyes stray for a moment to glance at her travel companion, and she comments on the new color of her bangs. "Red, huh?" she asks.

The attention makes Zoe happy. Without a second thought, she grabs the tinted pieces of hair between her fingers and twists them to show them off.

The fact Britt copied the same color Zoe picked to pay tribute to her mother bothers her, and she agitatedly squirms in her seat. Unable to hold her tongue, she awkwardly laughs. "Looks better on me," she says with a shrug.

Bending forward to take off her shoes, Britt pretends not to hear her. As she sits back up, her lungs exhale a sigh, and she extends her feet, stretching them out to rest on the dashboard.

Zoe glares at her from the corner of her eye. "Come on, dude. Get your gross feet off my dash."

The satisfaction of irritating her makes Britt smirk, and she throws her hands into the air with a chuckle. "Don't blow a gasket. That was a test." She places her feet back on the floor and taps Zoe's shoulder with her finger. "Had to make sure rehab hasn't changed you too much," she says. Seeing she isn't winning her over, she changes the subject. "Seriously, sometimes it's crazy how the universe works with timing."

The words oddly resonate with Zoe, almost like a déjà vu moment. Although she can't place her finger on what her gut is telling her, she feels she has lived this moment before; the thought makes her shiver.

In short order, their relationship dynamics pick up exactly where they left off before rehab. Britt scans the car, and her curious eyes stop on the fad-ed duffel bag in the backseat. She reaches inside and grabs the first item lying on top of it. "Whoa, what's happening here?" she asks, then grabs a bra and laughs. Her finger holds the undergarment into the air, letting it fly like a flag in the wind. "You live out of your car now?"

This is the first time Zoe has heard someone point out her homelessness, and she isn't ready to face that harsh reality. Though she pretends to have a hard exterior, the current circumstance of her life mortifies her, and each cruel word hits a nerve. Lifting a hand from the wheel, she snatches the bra away and throws it into the backseat. Her cheeks flush as she quickly attempts to justify her predicament. "So what if I am? Plenty of other people have done it."

As Zoe fumbles for a name, Britt moves past the topic, shifting her focus to checking her appearance in her visor mirror.

Smacking the steering wheel, Zoe blurts out the first person who comes to mind. "Like Jim Morrison! Prime fucking example, and look what happened to him. Sometimes shit happens, and you just got to go with the flow," she says with a smile. Immediately, she switches the subject. "Anyway, enough about my shit. Let's talk about you and why you're dressed like that in the middle of nowhere."

Enjoying the attention, Britt repositions herself to tell her friend what happened. "Oh girl, do I have a story for you. We have so much to catch up on," she says.

Zoe relaxes in the driver's seat, relieved that she's no longer the focus of interest.

Britt clears her throat to retell her dramatic account. "First, let me explain my outfit—or lack t hereof... I was heading to a music festival. Funny enough, it's the same one we were supposed to go to together."

Britt's apathetic delivery of the comment makes Zoe roll her eyes. "Oh, you mean before or after you fucking left me to die alone in rehab?" she asks. Irritated that she has disregarded her feelings and hasn't apologized, she glances at her friend to make eye contact. Met with silence, she clenches her jaw.

Acting like the point of contention doesn't exist, Britt continues, talking over her. "So back to my story. Your favorite person, Dale, had one of his usual episodes, and we got into it pretty bad." She reaches for the sleeve of her blue-butterfly-adorned flowing kimono and pulls it up to reveal a bruise on her left wrist. "The only difference was that I decided to fight back this time, just like *you* told me to do." Appearing defeated, she lifts her finger and points to herself. "So here I am, looking like a hitchhiking space hooker, stranded in the middle of nowhere."

Although she doesn't necessarily recall the conversation, she's automatically engulfed by a blanket of guilt over her friend's suffering at the hands of her advice.

As they sit in awkward silence, Britt adds to her manipulative ploy by pretending to sniffle and fight back the tears.

The tactic works. Zoe tries to make light of the situation to relieve her overwhelming remorse for getting angry at her. Peering at her, she jokingly chuckles. "You look fucking ridiculous," she states while trying to maintain her focus on driving.

Confident she has her right where she wants her, Britt switches off her pity ploy and checks her appearance in the mirror while applying more glitter lip gloss. When finished, she obnoxiously smacks her lips and blows kisses to her reflection.

Still concerned about hurting her friend's feelings, Zoe further attempts to gather forgiveness by making up for the hardship she caused. "You just gave me a killer idea. Maybe the music fest is what I need to get my mind off things. When you invited me, it gave me something to look forward to. Seriously, it was the only thing that kept me from offing myself in rehab, so I owe you one."

Hearing the news that she just scored a free ride to the festival is a bonus to Britt, and her face grows crazed with excitement. She lets out a loud gasp with an ear-shattering squeal. "Oh, my God! Yes! This'll be just like old times!" she says, reaching for her furry blue backpack.

Strangely, Zoe didn't remember Britt carrying it earlier, but she's intrigued nonetheless and tries to see what she's doing with it in the passenger seat.

As her hand digs deep into the mysterious bag, she bites her lip in concentration. "We have to celebrate... Damn, where did I put that?" Her face freezes as her fingertips fumble for what she's looking for.

The sound of the manic rustling makes Zoe anxious. "Put what?"

"Aha, there you are." Britt retracts her hand from her bag to showcase a small cocaine-spoon necklace shaped like a blue crystal. "Thankfully, I always carry an emergency stash," she says, waving it in front of Zoe's face.

Zoe hasn't been in the presence of drugs in a few months, and as the cocaine swings like a hypnotic pendulum in front of her eyes, she relives the taste. She struggles not to stare, and her jaw tightens as she fights the urge. Not wanting to be a buzzkill, she playfully goes along with her companion's excitement. "I almost forgot what the good stuff looks like," she says.

Retracting her hand from her face, Britt ogles her stash and motions to the side of the road. Her speech quickens to downplay the situation. "Let's pull over really quick and do a bump," she states. As she notices her friend's posture stiffen and her grip tighten around the leather steering wheel, she fears she has lost her drug buddy. "C'mon. It'll be fun; plus, it'll be like a twofer since you have to change anyway," she says. Her judgmental eyes slowly scan the outfit, and she snickers, further chipping away at her self-esteem. "You can't show up dressed like that."

The fact that she's being put in a compromising situation so soon after rehab irks her. As she weighs her options, she justifies pulling the car over to change. "I guess you're right," she says with a dramatic sigh so her friend doesn't feel she has won. As her eyes drift to the vial of white powder, saliva forms in her mouth. "My life has been pretty lame recently anyway, so I do deserve it," she states as she jerks the wheel, erratically yanking her car to the side of the road. She twists the key to turn off the engine, kicks her shoes off to get comfortable, sits on her feet, and turns to face her passenger.

Britt waits with her arm extended toward her, holding a spoonful of blow.

She wants the substance more than anything; its sight makes her jittery, and she unconsciously bites her lip.

As Britt waits for her to take it, her patience runs thin, and she shrugs. "Fine then." She pulls her hand back and snorts the substance.

Watching someone ingest the powder makes Zoe lose control, and she snaps. "Okay, hurry the fuck up and pass me some before I change my mind," she says.

Pretending to help her calm down, Britt waves her hand in a sweeping meditative motion in front of her paling face. "Ooosaaaa," she says.

As she's already filled with self-loathing over what she's about to do, the act makes her even more irritable.

Britt reads the tension and quickly scoops the snowy substance onto the spoon. "Seriously, you need to calm down and meditate more," she says.

Before her friend can extend the spoon, she eagerly snatches it from her and snorts the contents. A buzzing feeling travels through her blood, and a warm twitchiness prickles her skin. Wearing a huge smile, she wipes her nose and sucks the remnants from her fingernails.

Britt stares in awe at Zoe from the passenger side, impressed by her speedy ingestion and newfound enthusiasm. Lifting her fingers high in the air, she snaps them to simulate a round of applause and shouts, "Yas!" The high volume of her voice creates an echo in the desert's desolation. With a smile, she turns around to paw through the duffel bag in the backseat.

Zoe's eyes bulge as she feels a rush of energy. Flipping around in the driver's seat, she watches Britt choose an outfit. "What are we thinking?" Zoe asks.

Britt doesn't hide her disappointment with the contents of the bag. "Um, that these are all your clothes? What did you do, just throw random shit into a bag?"

Not thinking the selection is that bad, Zoe opens her mouth to give a rebuttal and is met with a wadded bikini top hitting her in the face.

"That's it! That's the winner!" Britt says.

Dazed by the swimwear hitting her nose, Zoe fumbles to grab the skimpy item that's fallen to her lap. She inspects it, analyzing the stripe pattern. Realizing Britt didn't choose anything for her to wear over it, she nervously laughs. "What is this? Lingerie?" she asks.

As her friend retreats to her seat to watch her change, she tosses the jean miniskirt to her. "Oh, my God, shut up! You are going to be fire!" she says.

Being so exposed makes her uncomfortable, and she turns around to look for another option.

Zoe's eyes roll as Britt barricades the backseat with her left arm to stop her, and she glances at the skirt sitting on her lap and the swim top in her hand. "Those are your clothes, so you can't get mad at what I picked. That's the best option you've got," she says.

Zoe feels pressured to please her friend and turns back around, facing forward in her seat. Taking a deep breath to calm her mind, she sizes up the clothing again and nervously stares at the bikini top.

Tired of her friend's shenanigans, Britt becomes impatient in the passenger seat. She wants her to hurry so they can head to the festival. "Don't think, just do," she says, snapping her fingers.

Even though Britt tries to rush her, Zoe still feels uneasy and looks over her shoulder to see if any cars are coming.

It makes Britt angry that they're wasting so much time, and her friendly demeanor snaps. "Now you're shy? What happened to that girl I used to know who was crowned the party queen?" Taking a moment of pause, she attempts to reel in the harshness of her rant and taps her finger against the tank top covering her heart. "I know the one who fucking stole Adam Schaffer's heart is still in there."

Hearing her crush's name makes Zoe smirk, and immediately she misses the good ol' days.

The sight of Zoe daydreaming makes Britt laugh. "Plus, dude, you're in the middle of nowhere, so I promise no one will see those itty-bitty titties of yours," she says as she watches her squirm. As soon as she notices the passive jab bothering Zoe, she dramatically turns around to give her privacy and, feeling accomplished, smirks.

All Zoe wants to do is please her only friend. Before allowing herself to second-guess her decision, she gives in to the pressure. "Fine! Geez! I'm changing," she says and begins to remove her shirt in hopes she'll stop tormenting her.

As the tank top lifts from her skin, Britt glances over her shoulder and notices a sizable purplish-blue bruise on her rib cage next to her bony spine. Not wanting Zoe to waste any more of her time away from the festival, she ignores the injury and turns her back to rummage through her bag. Checking again to make sure she's still distracted with changing, she sneaks a bottle of pills out of her purse and quietly takes two. Just as she zips her bag back up, she hears a commotion in the driver's seat and turns to look.

Zoe spins around to show off her friend's clothing selection and throws her hands into the sky to innocently pose as if revealing a magic trick. "Voila! Happy now?"

Experiencing jitters from the combination of substances, Britt's body shakes and her hands neurotically clap, applauding Zoe's outfit.

The enthusiastic response makes Zoe more comfortable in her skin, and she embraces the scantily clad attire. Lifting her hand, she winks and forms her fingers into the shape of a gun to make a joke. "Next time I'm charging for the strip show," she says.

Britt makes obnoxious hooting and hollering noises as her friend takes a bow. "Brava! Brava!" she says. Pinching her fingers together, she kisses them and throws her hand into the sky to further laud her masterpiece. "You realize if we see Adam at this thing, he'll die when he sees how hot you look," she says, her eyes spastically darting at every noise the breeze carries.

Hearing her crush's name again makes Zoe grin, and the thought of seeing his face fills her body with a warm sensation.

As Zoe zones out, Britt is on a mission to keep the party going. "This calls for another celebration!" she says. Not skipping a beat, she rummages through her bag and retrieves a small bottle of tequila. Before taking a sip, she extends the bottle to Zoe. "Take a shot for good luck, and you can't say no, because I went through a lot to swipe this from my dad's liquor cabinet."

The sound of the sloshing alcohol knocks Zoe back to reality, and she politely declines the offer. As she pushes the bottle back, she makes a joke to lighten the mood. "Whoa, Silver. Aren't we a little hasty? Shouldn't we wait until we get there?" she asks with an awkward laugh.

Britt's eyes dramatically roll. "Don't be a baby. Seriously, girl, I miss the old you," she says, setting the bottle on her friend's lap. She points to the bottle and glares at her. "You won't die from one sip."

The sensation of the glass bottle against her bare legs makes Zoe's heart skip a beat. Overcome with guilt over relapsing on cocaine, she mentally justifies the decision she's about to make. Her eyes nervously glance at Britt's uncomfortable stare, and not wanting to disappoint her, she snatches the bottle and chokes back a hefty gulp. Zoe's face squinches from the alcohol's burn. She looks away, pretending her break from soberness never happened as she passes the bottle back to Britt.

"And she's back!" Britt proclaims, grasping the bottle with a massive grin. Following suit, she takes a shot to commemorate the occasion.

The sound of the liquid swirling in the bottle makes Zoe want to flee. As she reaches for her car keys, she catches a glimpse of her sobriety keychain and her entire body tenses with hatred. "I never fucking left," she says under her breath. Wanting to escape from her haunting decisions, she tries to start the car.

Instead of the usual start-up roar, they're met with the sound of a flooded engine.

Zoe tries a few more times, but the car won't start. She loses her composure and pushes herself back from the steering wheel. "Fuck, you've gotta be shitting me!" she screams as she slams her fists against the dash.

Just as Britt is about to take another swig of tequila, the violent outburst catches her attention, and she pauses to stare in disbelief.

Zoe aggressively swings the car door open, jumps onto her bare feet, and kicks dust into the air to let off steam.

The dramatic charade amuses Britt, and as she hears the door slam shut, she leisurely takes another swig from the bottle.

While beating herself up over her poor choices, Zoe paces the length of the car to collect her thoughts. Releasing a grunt, she eyes the sky. "I feel like someone is punishing me from above," she mutters.

Still enjoying the view from the passenger's seat, Britt shifts her eyes slowly and scans the clouds to see what she's talking about. Tired of her friend being a buzzkill, she shrugs and gets out of the car. "Okay, dramatic much?" she asks. With a laugh, she continues. "Looks like we're walking."

Chapter Twelve

OLD HABITS DIE HARD

As Britt shuts the car door, she loses her balance and almost falls. She laughs as she steadies herself and looks over the top of the car at her friend. "I know something that will help," she says. Seeing she's caught Zoe's attention, she leans over the vehicle and shakes the tequila bottle at her.

Wanting something to take away her spiraling depression, Zoe accepts the peace offering and takes a swig. This time, rather than cringe from the harshness of the alcohol, she enjoys the pain caused by the poison—punishing herself feels good. She smirks and passes the bottle back. "Tag! You're it!" she states.

Pleased by Zoe's newfound amenable personality, Britt takes a swig while enjoying the moment. "You realize we're not that far," she says. As she looks into the horizon, her eyes squint. "Just before I was rudely kicked out of the car, I saw a sign for the festival. It said it was only ten miles away, and that was back where you scooped me." Her body happily twirls, and she takes a few steps forward. "So, if we keep following the road, we should be there in no time."

Watching Britt's certainty grow brings Zoe comfort, and having nothing to lose, she follows Britt's gaze down the road toward their destination. She spontaneously throws her hands up. "Fuck it. Let's do it," she says, leaning over the side of the open convertible, she unzips her backpack.

Zoe's willingness to comply shocks Britt, who runs back to give her a high five. "That's the spirit!" Britt says.

Zoe stuffs a few things she needs into her pack and, in the process, notices the picture of her mother she took from her room. Smiling now, and redirecting her attention, she finds a pair of slip-on boots and pulls them on. She shifts her weight, swinging the backpack straps over her shoulders, then returns her waiting friend's high five. "Okay, let's rage," Zoe says, then turns and heads down the road. Realizing Britt isn't following, she turns to see her frozen in place with a gawp of surprise. "Are you coming?" she asks.

Britt, still computing that Zoe has taken the lead, remains glued to her spot.

Zoe laughs at her stunned face and sarcastically summons her to catch up with her waving hands. "Hurry up, loser. I don't have all day," she says, exuding a mocking tone.

Even though she loves to instigate insecurities by poking fun at others, Britt doesn't like to be the butt of anyone's joke. As a smirk forms on her lips, she musters a comment that'll dig at her core. With a grin that carries a hint of anger, she cackles. "Dude, what's the big hurry. It's not like you have anything better to do, you're homeless," she states with disgust.

Her comment triggers Zoe's underlying shame and embarrassment. Trying to brush her words off, she shrugs to pretend she isn't bothered and turns her back to her to walk.

Rather than take offense at her friend for ignoring her, Britt allows the situation to fuel her ego. Thinking it's funny to watch her squirm, she continues to spew taunting comments. "Big kid on campus, huh?" she shouts.

Pretending the words aren't bothering her, Zoe twirls her hands to the sides like helicopter blades to further express that she doesn't care. "Yeah, whatever. Cool your jets, man," she says to deescalate Britt's toxic ego.

They both laugh.

As Britt runs to catch up, Zoe's steps turn into a strut, and she uses the road as her runway. Quickening her pace, Britt passes her friend and blows her a competitive kiss.

Zoe giggles at her goofy behavior and joins in the model-like processional to pass the time. A breeze kicks up some sand near their feet, and as she glances down to look at it, she becomes self-conscious of her lack of clothing. Putting the fault on Britt for her outfit selection, she masks her insecurity by poking fun at their attire. "People will think we're hookers," she says, her hands awkwardly running up and down her body.

Britt takes the nervous gesture as a huge compliment and laughs at the remark as she peers down to admire her seductive presentation. The sight of her space-oddity-inspired denim selection makes her confidence unstoppable. She embraces every aspect of herself and displays her arrogance by dramatically flipping her hair. She clears her throat and adjusts her cleavage. "Well, then..." She grins as she playfully sneaks up behind Zoe and pulls the strings of her top untying them.

Almost being exposed makes Zoe scream, and her hands clutch her chest to cover herself. As she fumbles to retie the strings, she laughs at her friend's ridiculousness.

Britt runs ahead of Zoe and turns around, walking backward to face her. With a smile, she holds out her thumb to seductively hitchhike. "Come on. Let's give 'em a show," she states.

Looking around to see if anyone's watching, Zoe is relieved to find pure isolation and freedom. Without a soul in sight, she joins in and gives her best stripper walk. Her backpack slouches to her elbows as her body playfully spins. Suddenly she notices something out of her peripheral and freezes dead in her tracks as she tries to make out what the object is. "You've gotta be shitting me," she says, as the headlights of a large van approaching a mile down the road come into view.

She rubs her eyes to make sure it's not a mirage. Her heart races. Nervous that the vehicle's occupants might have witnessed her behavior and have gotten the wrong idea, she crosses her arms to hide her body. "Is the desert getting to me, or is that a van?" she asks, stammering as her hand reaches to get Britt's attention.

The idea of not having to walk any further excites Britt, whose feet are blistered. Leaving Zoe frozen in place, she races toward the approaching headlights, hoping to land a ride. Pausing briefly, she turns and shouts to Zoe. "Push your tits together, bitch! We could get out of here!" On a mission, Britt fluffs her hair and adjusts her outfit to show more cleavage. Her eyes glance back, signaling for Zoe to follow. "Flirt like your life depends on it! Let's see if we can get a ride," she states, giving her an encouraging look.

This being her first encounter with another vehicle in a long time, and its appearance in such a remote location paralyzes Zoe with confusion.

The setting sun reveals the van's exterior aesthetics as the vehicle gains speed, barreling toward them. Circling the indigo blue exterior is a tan stripe and random dings embedded in the metal. The windows are darkly tinted, making it impossible to discern who's driving. Splattered winged bugs of different shapes and sizes decorate the windshield, grille, and headlights. An assortment of faded rainbow- and sunshine-themed stickers adorn each door, and the interior side of every window dons tattered navy floral curtains.

An uneasy feeling stirs in Zoe's stomach as she stays behind and watches the beat-up van pull up next to Britt. She tries to voice her opinion, but her trembling fear causes each word to become softer than expected. "Wait..." she says.

Slowly the van rolls to a stop, creating a screech that cuts the stagnant air. The passenger window rolls down.

Britt takes a flirtatious skip toward the vehicle, leans toward the open window, and begins chatting with the concealed individual.

As Zoe observes the scene unfold from a distance, the sound of the vehicle's loud exhaust infiltrates her eardrums and stimulates her anxiety. Crossing her arms, she glances around the surrounding desert to determine escape options in case the driver attempts to abduct them. The sound of Britt's cackling laughter pierces the white noise of the exhaust, and her racing glance lands on her companion.

Simultaneously, Britt turns her head, making eye contact, and she smiles. The alcohol has made her loopy as its effects set in with the prior substances. As her feet stagger, she catches her balance on the van and shouts at Zoe with slurred speech. "Oh, my God, you won't believe this, but he wants you!"

She can't understand a single word her friend is chattering. Raising her hand to her ear, she mimes a sign for her to talk louder.

Getting the hint, Britt holds up her index finger. "One sec," she says. Smiling, she shifts her attention back to the driver. Her eyes grow wide with excitement like she's won the jackpot. She turns toward Zoe and tries to focus on her steps to maintain her seductive prowess while racing back to fill her in.

As she watches her friend approach, she nervously taps her foot, and her limbs fidget. Impatient with her staggering pace and wanting the situation to be over, Zoe quickly walks to meet her halfway to get the details. All she wants is to hear some good news and noticing her smile, she assumes the conversation went well. "What did he say? Can he give us a ride?"

The question makes Britt's smile grow wide as she prepares for the grand reveal. She twirls in a circle; her feet land facing Zoe, and she taps her nose. "He wants you!" she states exuberantly, her words projecting much louder than necessary.

Avoiding eye contact, Zoe nervously tries to decipher what she means, and having no luck, she gives her a dumbfounded look. "Wait—uh, what?" she asks.

She laughs at her naive confusion. "Like, he, bow-chick-a-wow-wow wants you," she says as she thrusts her hips to give a clue.

The provocative gesture makes her eyebrows lift in a look of shock.

Britt nudges her shoulder to make her relax.

Zoe crosses her arms to cover her cleavage and aggressively shakes her head. "No way. No way in hell," she states. Not wanting to wait for her friend's response or deal with peer pressure, she turns and starts to walk in the opposite direction of the van.

Britt thinks Zoe isn't being as grateful as she should be and, seeing that she isn't stopping, chases after her. Eyeing the large bruise on her back, she targets it by grabbing her waist at its precise location.

Zoe winces from the pain and smacks her hand away. The intentional cruelty puts her at her wit's end, and she turns to confront her. "You know what? Fuck you! I'm done. This little adventure is over," she says. Her eyes well with tears from the exhaustion of her life's dealings. She concludes that everyone in her life has deceived her somehow, and at that moment, any inkling of optimism dies in her body.

Playing into Zoe's vulnerable state, Britt grabs her arm and peers into her eyes. "You know, he's actually kind of cute... Besides, we'll need the money; we're almost out of blow." Quickly, she realizes her choice of words may come across as insensitive and tries to make the situation seem like a team effort. "I would fuck him if I were in your shoes; I tried, but he said he didn't want me. He wants *you*, so you're the only hope we've got." Adding to her manipulative ploy, she feigns empathy by softening her expression.

Troubled by her words, Zoe remains quiet as her glance alternates between the idle vehicle and the only friend in her life.

Britt grabs her face to regain her attention. "Girl, come on. You're living out of your car, and I don't know where the fuck my boyfriend is. Let's get real. How are we going to pay for our shit? We need cash, and that guy has it."

Hearing the depressing reality forces Zoe to acknowledge her dire circumstance and makes it impossible to continue to avoid ignoring the truth. She has no choice—she needs the money. Her lip quivers with sadness over the decision she knows she must make. She tightly crosses her arms and tries to make light of the situation to make it feel consensual. "You said he's hot, right?" she asks.

Britt doesn't feel a single ounce of sympathy for her sadness; instead, her eyes light up with excitement and the fact that she's getting what she wants wipes any ounce of concern from her face. After hearing the question, she silently looks into Zoe's eyes and, making the sign of the cross with her hand, kisses her fist to make a promise. "Yes, bitch!" she exclaims.

Concerned over dragging down her mood or disappointing her, she attempts to appear unbothered by cracking her twitching lips into a grin. Wanting to get the obligation over with, she glances over her shoulder at the waiting van and extends her hand.

As Zoe's fingers stretch through the air, Britt reads her mind and, reaching into her fuzzy blue bag, pulls out the partial bottle of tequila. "A little liquid courage," she says, placing it in her hand.

Still fixated on her impending fate, she lets her eyes drift to the smoke fumes pouring from the van's exhaust pipe as she pops off the top and chugs the rest of the bottle. She drops the empty glass to the ground and, feeling dead inside, staggers toward the vehicle.

Britt picks up the bottle and makes sure no drops are left before turning to watch her walk away. Worried the sight of the juvenile decorations on her backpack will reveal her age, she quickly does damage control and chases after Zoe. "Wait! Let me take your stuff!" she says.

Not looking back, Zoe drops her yellow backpack from her shoulders to the ground and continues to walk to the van.

Britt races to the bag and, seeing the bottom is covered in dust, refrains from picking it up. Not wanting to get dirty, she leaves it on the ground and uses it as a seat to give her feet a rest. As she makes herself comfortable, she waves to Zoe with a smile. "I'll be waiting here!" she says.

The ingested tequila enters her bloodstream, causing a warm blanket to engulf her body and the spark that once resided behind her irises to dull. Seeing no reason to acknowledge the driver through the open window, she walks directly to the door that leads to the backseat. Her body is numb, and her soul void of life, as she robotically goes through the motions of opening the vintage vehicle's heavy door. She doesn't look back.

Seeing her friend get inside excites Britt. While perched on the backpack, she daydreams about the money they'll soon have. Her trance is broken by the sound of the van door closing. "Make me proud!" she cheers.

A long while passes, and the setting sun vanishes below the horizon.

As Britt waits for her friend to exit with their money, she becomes bored and rummages through her furry bag for more goodies. Not wanting her buzz to end, she pops open the prescription bottle and removes two white oblong pills. Chuckling to herself, she swallows them. "Now it's a party," she says, placing the bottle back in her bag. Just as she finishes zipping her purse, she hears the loud click of the van door, and her head snaps up to look. The view is blocked by the open door and hides everything happening until Zoe's feet hit the ground. Britt springs to her feet, impatient to find out how much money she made.

Zoe steps around the door and slams it shut. Her appearance is disheveled, her eyes bewildered. She straightens her skirt as she turns to face Britt. Even though she's traumatized, she takes a deep breath and puts on a happy face. As her eyes lift to observe her friend approaching, the van peels out next to her, making her jump.

The sight of their ride to the festival speeding away shifts Britt's attention. Carelessly leaving Zoe's belongings on the ground, she chases her while yelling at the top of her lungs. "Wait! What about our ride?"

As she watches Britt beeline past her, she takes a moment to finish buttoning her skirt and rubs a bruise that's forming on her left wrist. Still dazed, she watches the taillights get smaller in the distance. The fact that her friend is more concerned with the fleeing vehicle than her well-being agitates her. After reaching into her swim top, she pulls out a small wad of cash. She then waves it into the air to get Britt's attention. "I got the money," she slurs.

When Britt hears that, along with the crinkling sound of the fanning bills, she spins around. The sight of the money triggers her to race to her friend, and she immediately snatches the green cluster from her trembling hand to count it.

Britt's greedy behavior irritates her, and the sight of the only meaningful possession she has left, carelessly tossed on the ground, angers her. Briefly, she shifts her attention to collect her backpack and clenches her jaw as she brushes the dust off it.

Ignoring Zoe's hostility, Britt continues counting the cash. She smiles widely, exposing a mouth of pearly whites, the light from the stars above reflecting off each one. The glistening exposed teeth mimic those of a snarling wolf. Even though it's only roughly a hundred dollars, it's more than she expected, and she shouts over her shoulder as she gasps. "Bitch, holy shit! Look at all this!" She holds the bills, spreads them as a fan, and waves them toward her face like a socialite on a hot summer's day. "I don't even want to know what you had to do for this, but I have to say, I love the slutty money," she states with a laugh. Infatuated by the cash, she no longer cares if she gets a little dusty and sits on the ground to enjoy the moment.

Zoe stares at her in disbelief.

As Britt sniffs each bill, she plans how they'll spend it. "Dude, we can roll for a month with this cash," she says.

Infuriated by Britt's behavior, she slings the strap of her backpack over her shoulder and races to snatch the money from her hand. "You mean, *I* can roll for a month," she states, shoving the bills into the front pocket of her bag. The harsh reality of what she just did to earn the money sets in, and her self-esteem disintegrates. Feeling the loneliest she has ever felt, she just wants someone to be there for her, and in a depressed daze, she slowly sits on the ground next to her travel companion.

Pouting and still annoyed by the money being taken from her, Britt refuses to give her eye contact.

Traumatized and not wanting to relive the graphic details of the ordeal, Zoe gives just enough information to garner the emotional support she yearns for. Leaning back on her hands, she accidentally places too much weight on her left wrist, which sends pain shooting up her arm. As she adjusts her body to get comfortable, she clutches the fresh bruise to stop the pain. "Yeah, that guy was a dick," she says, blankly staring forward.

When Brit finally glances at the area she's clutching, she notices the purple markings, but rather than show concern, she pulls up her sleeve, exposing her left wrist, and flashes her similar discoloration. "Welcome to the club," she says. Annoyed that Zoe is despondent, Britt rolls her eyes and rummages through her bag to retrieve two cigarettes. "Here. You need to take one of these and chill out," she says, handing her a Marlboro.

Zoe glances at the offering. She then grabs the smoke with her shaking hand and puts it in her mouth without saying a word.

Britt places the other between her lips to free her hands, then digs through her purse for a lighter. She leans toward Zoe and lights her cig, then lights her own. She takes a deep inhalation and blows a smoke ring, and her face relaxes. "A good smoke makes any rainy day better. That's what my mom always used to say," she says.

Britt's comment lightens Zoe's mood and makes her smirk. She takes a large puff of nicotine; a moment later, her lungs release a deep exhalation.

"Amen to that. She sounds like a smart woman," she says.

Not looking at each other, they sit in silence.

The quietness makes Zoe swirl in her thoughts, and she can't help but think back to the encounter with the driver of the van. Rather than shedding a tear over the disturbing experience, she breaks into an uncontrollable fit of laughter.

Even though Britt finds her behavior immature, she pretends to care in the hopes of silencing her so she can enjoy her smoke. "What now?" she asks.

Still numb from the ordeal, Zoe doesn't answer the question, but it breaks her stream of giggles. "I can't believe I just fucked some random guy." As she pauses, the reality of her experience sets in and she attempts to mask her self-loathing by trying to play it cool. While she mentally replays the horrific memory, she verbally dismisses her true feelings about the situation by brushing it off as nothing. "On the side of the road. I just fucked someone, on the side of the road, in the middle of nowhere. That's wild," she states. Her joking expression slowly dissipates from her face, and her eyes are left with an empty appearance.

Tired of hearing about her friend's encounter, Britt shrugs and takes another drag. Focusing on her wedged heels, she digs them into the dust. "We've all done worse," she states.

Zoe's thoughts swirl with self-condemnation, her body void of feeling as she puffs on her cigarette.

Wanting to change the subject, Britt uses her furry bag as a pillow and lies flat on the ground while finishing her cig and watching the stars.

Seeing Britt's body leave her peripheral vision triggers Zoe's fear of abandonment, and she peers beside her to make sure she's still there. Yearning to feel the same relaxation as her friend and forget about her tribulations, she moves her backpack to rest her head and joins her. The sensation of lying flat on the ground brings her some calmness.

The stars glow brightly above, their perfection against the clear night sky mimicking a painting. Each whimsical glistening light effortlessly floats in the pitch-black and removes the girls' worry. They both gaze up to admire the unforgettable view.

Britt clears her throat and puts her cigarette out on the ground beside her. "Isn't it beautiful?" she asks.

Following suit, Zoe refrains from looking away from the stars' luster and tamps her smoldering butt out in the sand. Fixated on the sky's aesthetics, she reminisces about her childhood. "Man..." Usually not being one to share, she pauses, second-guessing whether to disclose her thoughts. Tired of worrying about how others perceive her, she relinquishes control and lowers her defensive walls. "I haven't done this since I was little. My dad and I used to lie on the grass in the yard. We wouldn't say a single word—we'd just stare up at the stars, enjoying the moment together." The thought of how things have drastically changed since that innocent time fills her with sadness, and she awkwardly chuckles to cover it. She smiles as she grasps the one good memory she seemed to have forgotten over the years. "Honestly, that's probably the last decent memory I have of my childhood," she says. As she continues her introspective reflection, she gains a new understanding, and the resentment she once felt toward her father is replaced by forgiveness. "Yeah, it all kind of went to shit when my mom died." Talking about her mother's passing out loud makes her body tense.

Even though she doesn't feel like being someone's therapist, Britt pretends to act concerned to allow her friend to process the epiphany. "How did she die?" she asks.

Always having internally denied the autopsy results provided by the coroner and the circumstance in which her mother was found, Zoe pauses to gather enough strength to talk about it. To manage her emotions, she refrains from shifting her head and directs her attention to a single star. She takes a deep centering breath and opens her mouth to speak. "Overdose... Benzos."

Britt tilts her head to look at her.

Feeling her friend's eyes on her causes Zoe's emotional floodgates to open, allowing years of pent-up feelings to pour out. "I've never told anyone this, but I was the one who found her. I still remember every detail like it was yesterday. I was just a kid. I got up early on a Sunday to watch cartoons and noticed my mom wasn't up like usual to make breakfast. It was never anything fancy, just the basics, toast, or a bowl of cold cereal. Regardless, I went into her room because I was hungry. That's where I found her. She was lying there peacefully in bed; I swear to God, I thought she was sleeping, so I closed the door to let her rest." She continues to share the memory as she fights back her tears. "I had no idea anything was wrong. It was several hours later before my dad got home from mowing lawns for extra cash. He asked why my mom wasn't watching me, and I told him she was sleeping. Like a fucking dumbass, I thought she was sleeping... You should have seen how he looked at me; it's like he immediately connected the dots that I couldn't. Sometimes I still wonder if it's my fault that she's not alive since I stupidly thought she was just sleeping in," she says.

As tears run down her cheeks, she clears her throat. "The craziest thing is that my father never mentioned to the police that I was the one who found her. I always thought it was because we didn't have insurance, and it was just a money thing if they said I needed therapy, but I think he was trying to protect me."

Hearing the sadness in her voice, Britt attempts to reach out to touch her hand to give her some sort of reassurance that everything is okay.

Not wanting to be touched, Zoe pulls away.

Put off by her friend denying her attempt at showing some form of compassion, Britt withdraws her hand. Staring back up at the stars, she changes the subject. "It sure is incredible," she says, then closes her eyes and releases a meditative breath. She takes in the serenity of the moment. "It's so peaceful out here. I feel so Zen."

Realizing her rejection may have come across as harsh, Zoe expresses appreciation for her company. "I'm happy you were hitchhiking today. When I saw you, I didn't know what to do with my life. I was driving to nowhere," she says.

Britt's eyes open, and she rolls over to face her. "Me too."

The exchange confirms that the feeling is reciprocated, and Zoe shifts to look at her. "Let's swear we will always stay together and never forget this moment."

Britt's demeanor becomes serious. "Never," she says, extending her pinky.

They both smirk as they pinky shake to seal the deal.

Upon their finger's release, Britt sits up and rummages through her bag. She sticks out her tongue in concentration while blindly fumbling through its contents.

Thinking her friend might need help with what she's doing, Zoe offers to assist her. As she leans toward her to help, she hears what sounds like pills tumbling within the plastic walls of a prescription bottle.

Britt's eyes fill with excitement as she hears the familiar clatter while pulling the prescription bottle from her purse. Its contents are no mystery to her as she's accessed them several times during their desert journey. She playfully shakes them and listens closely, as if counting how many remain. After quickly popping open the cap, she shakes a white pill into the palm of her hand and holds it out to Zoe.

The sight of the familiar shape and bared lines horrifies her, and her body freezes. "Is that what I think it is?" she stammers.

Taking Zoe's apprehension as masked excitement, Britt smiles and nods while waving the pill in front of her eyes.

Not knowing how to process the situation, she reluctantly takes it between her two fingers and her heart races. "I just told you benzos killed my mom," she says.

Listening to Zoe bring up her painful past again annoys Britt. She becomes defensive at her lack of appreciation for what she's offering, and seeing no problem with the situation, she views Zoe's statements as a buzz kill to the happy moment. She condemns her ungrateful behavior as she shakes a second one onto her flat palm for herself. "Girl, you aren't your mom; you know your limits," she says.

Worried her only friend might abandon her like her mother, Zoe stares at the pill as she attempts to relinquish her fear. "That's fucked," she says under her breath. Her eyes dart to glance at Britt as she swallows the tablet.

"See? So easy," Britt says with a smirk.

Again, Zoe looks at the pill in her hand; then, closing her eyes, she places it on her tongue and swallows it. A short while later, the drug kicks in, and everything blurs around her. Embracing the peacefulness of her spiraling daze, she slowly lays her head back down on her backpack and shuts her eyes.

Chapter Thirteen

TIME FOR THE FESTIVAL

The sun begins to rise across the desert terrain. Each ray of warm orange light that successfully breaks through the clouds illuminates the lids of Zoe's closed eyes. The skin of her eyelids flutters as her mind remains in a deep REM cycle. A dozen or so crows fly overhead and loudly squawk as they pass by.

The shrill commotion knocks her from her deep slumber, and she feels confused and dizzy from the combination of substances. Her eyes slowly open, and her head throbs as she sits up to stretch her arms. Typically, when she took a similar dosage in the past, she felt more alert the morning after. She chalks it up to the fact that her couple of months of sobriety weakened her tolerance. Finishing her lengthy stretch, she turns her attention to wake her companion so they won't be late for the festival, but something doesn't feel right.

Britt's head rests peacefully on her furry pillow purse. Her eyes are open, her limbs stiff.

Ignoring the oddness of her position, Zoe leans closer, shaking Britt's shoulders to wake her. "It's time to go to the festival," she says. Not receiving a response, she tries again, this time more forcefully. Panicked that she isn't responding, she frantically searches around her body and notices the open prescription bottle from the night before resting in her open palm. The rest of the pills lay scattered around her.

She picks one up to confirm she's not seeing things and feeling the texture between her fingers causes reality to set in. "Fuck!" Connecting the dots of the horrifying situation, she frantically looks around, scanning the horizon for anyone who might be able to help, but is met with only the desert's isolation. Hysterical, she springs to her feet and, cupping her hands around her mouth, screams as loud as her lungs allow. "Help! Someone, please help!" Her voice echoing against the open terrain causes her mind to shut down, and she falls to her knees. Hovering over Britt, she desperately tries to help her, but her body is cold to the touch, her lips dark blue. Zoe's attempts are futile—Britt is dead.

Terrified to be alone, she continues to shake her and shouts louder. "Britt! Britt, please, no. Please wake up." Clutching her icy palm in her hand, she touches it to her face, hoping to feel a human connection. "Don't do this to me, Britt," she says, checking her wrist for a pulse. Her expression shifts to one of horror and dropping Britt's hand to the ground, she sobs uncontrollably. In an angry outburst, she pushes her unresponsive body with her palms and burrows her head into her torso. "You can't leave me. Everyone fucking leaves me. Don't do this to me." She hyperventilates as tears stream down her cheeks onto her friend's lifeless body. "You're right: I'm not my mom. Please wake up," she says, burying her head in her hands.

At the height of her hysterics, she feels the sensation of her heart being ripped from her rib cage, and breathing becomes difficult. The excruciating pain causes her to sit up, and clutching her chest, she tightly closes her eyes, hoping it will go away. Her throat tightens in a suffocating squeeze, and she's convinced the terrifying ordeal has stemmed a horrific panic attack. She refrains from looking at the ground for fear of seeing her deceased friend's body. Even though she is unable to fully push through the horrible feeling, she manages to build enough courage and opens her eyes to face her reality.

⊰•——◆——•⊱

Terror and confusion overcome her as she finds she doesn't recognize her surroundings. The terrain has shifted from one of complete desolation to an expansive space generously intermixed with desert flora and tumbleweeds. There's no road to lead her path, and though a large cluster of Joshua trees obstructs her view, she can make out what resembles a significant stage in the distance.

The unfamiliar scenery makes her feel out of control and on the verge of insanity as the suffocating symptoms worsen. Her body slips into a state of shock, the lack of oxygen hunches her over as if she's bowing in prayer. As she gasps for air, she catches another glimpse of the corpse lying on the ground, and her face turns pale.

It too has shifted with the change of scenery.

She tries to use what little energy she has left to crawl nearer to the body. As her shaking limbs weaken, her eyes widen with insurmountable fear as she attains a closer view. The red-streaked hair is knotted into two space buns that are much smaller than she remembered. A neon-colored festival band hangs loosely from the skinny frail wrist and even though the festival make-up is identical, the clothing is not.

The same eyes that were once a window to a soul now hold a lifeless gaze that offers no reflection. At once, she's flooded with all the pain attributed to the horrible atrocities she has suffered in her short seventeen years of life.

Hovering above the corpse, she is now face-to-face with her worst nightmare.

It is her.

Running out of oxygen, she can only whisper a few fear-driven words under her breath as she continues to fixate on her body's eerie details.

"No, please, I'm not ready," she cries, releasing a single dust-laden tear. No longer wishing to view the corpse, she struggles to close her eyes and is met with a stinging sensation. They're stuck, and she's forced to look at herself lying on the ground. Convulsions overcome her, and a debilitating raw pain travels from her chest to her throat as she regurgitates a foamy substance. She tries to stop vomiting, but the choking only worsens. As her hands press against the dirt to stabilize herself, her gaze falls back to her dreaded remains. A half-dried bile-colored matter is crusted over her blueish-purple lips and is the same color as the substance foaming from her mouth.

She lets out an uncontrollable cough as she collapses forward, landing face-to-face with her deceased self.

Drops of blood fall into the crevice between the corpse's nose and top lip, and as she lifts her hand to feel where they came from, she loses her balance and tumbles to her side. As she lies there with her gaping eyes, she scans the lifeless body beside her.

Zoe hears the sound of cars pulling in to park as people trickle into the festival. A group of friends, drinking from plastic cups, walks near the stage on the other side of the Joshua trees that obscure her view.

As she hears their laughter, a gust of wind blows an empty cup across the field, and it lands inches from her hand. She tries to scream for help with all her might, but her voice has been silenced. Helpless and face-to-face with the cruelty of her fate, she takes her last gasp of dust-filled air and makes one final attempt to get up but only rolls into her corpse. Rather than feel the coldness of the physical body, she feels herself become one with her reality, and with one last convulsion, everything goes limp.

Chapter Fourteen

LIFE GOES ON

At the desert venue's front gate, festival go-ers wait with their wristbands on to check into day two of the party. The scene is complete chaos; everyone mingles and shares their thoughts about the musical artists they're excited to see perform that day, party experiences, and the exclusive events they've been invited to. It's like spring break on steroids, but rather than just college-aged kids being in attendance, the age range of the participants spans multiple generations. As people are let in, more arrive. An assortment of vehicles and RVs kick up dust as they're directed to their designated parking areas.

A giant bug hits the windshield of a white jeep as it slowly travels down the long dirt road to park, and as it splatters across the glass, the two girls in the car scream at the top of their lungs. Both look to be in their early twenties. Even though they aren't related, they appear to be twins. Their bleached-blond extensions are identical wavy curls with small, braided strands intermixed with their bangs. Each of their complexions has a tan tone that matches the color of a pumpkin spice latte, and though their faces might not have matched when they were younger, their extensive facial fillers make them look like clones.

Still freaking out over the bug splatter, the girl driving the car closes her eyes while pushing the button next to her steering wheel to spray wiper fluid onto the windshield.

They catch their breath as the bug vanishes with the wipers' rhythmic motion.

Immediately the blonde in the passenger's seat turns to her driving friend and, taking a deep breath, places her hand on her shoulder. "Oh, my God, Chelsea. You just saved us," she says.

The fact that she's a hero makes Chelsea proud of her accomplishment, and as she turns into the area to park, she smiles. "Shut the fuck up, Becky.

You know I'd take a bullet for you," she says, pulling into her directed spot and putting the car in park.

As soon as she shuts off the engine, they hop out of the jeep and stand next to each other, their mouths dropping open in awe at their surroundings.

Becky takes out her phone and starts a live feed on her social media to document their arrival for their followers. After flipping the camera to face herself, she checks her appearance and waves. "So we just got here, and let me tell you, we're in love!" She turns the camera to her friend to get her opinion.

Chelsea sticks out her tongue and twirls. "Everything feels like a dream!" she exclaims. "I want to thank my sponsors for inviting me here; you're amazing, and so are my followers who are along with me on this epic journey!" Becky says.

As they are some of the first to arrive for the day, the parking area is relatively empty, with a random assortment of scattered cars. A muted yellow Volkswagen Beetle is parked diagonally from their spot, with the top retracted down, showcasing its cream-colored leather interior.

As Chelsea scans the parking area for places for them to take selfies to post on social media, she spots the large plastic eyelashes on the hood of the parked Volkswagen and points with a squeal of excitement. "OMG, that is so cute!" she says, running to get a closer look.

Not wanting to miss out on a fabulous photo opportunity, Becky follows with her live video still on. She skips to the car and speaks to her viewers. "I already know what I'll be doing this entire week-end." Lowering her voice, she pretends to whisper to them. "Chasing her," she says as she flips the camera to show her friend petting the stiff fake eyelashes glued to the headlights.

Mid rub, Chelsea closes her eyes for a moment to soak in the atmosphere. Taking a deep breath to center herself, she holds out her hand. "Crystal me, bitch," she says.

While filming the video, Becky reaches into a vel-vet purple satchel tied around her waist and pulls out a piece of rose quartz. She then runs to her friend's side and places the light-pink object in her hand. Next, she pulls a small bundle of sage out of the bag, lights it, then waves it around the area.

With the rose quartz in her palm, she smells the burning sage and tries to fan it toward herself. "Yes, girl, we must cleanse and rid ourselves of any negative thoughts so we can make this the best day ever," she says.

As the piece of sage slowly burns out, Becky hears soft music and looks around. "Do you hear that song?" she asks.

"It's a low-key kind of banger! Where's it coming from?" she says, moving her head to the beat.

Scanning for the source, Becky continues to film her live feed as they dance to the track. "Found it!" Noticing the driver's side door to the little convertible has been left ajar, she climbs into the driver's seat. "It's coming from the radio!" She gets comfortable and scans around to see if anyone is headed toward the abandoned vehicle. Seeing no one, she opens the glove compartment, finds a pair of yellow ombre-tinted sunglasses, and puts them on.

Chelsea turns on her phone's camera to start duel live videoing and zooms in on the car's eyelashes as she dances. "Turn that shit up, girl!" she commands Becky.

Hearing her friend's request, Becky acts as the DJ and turns up the tunes.

"To everyone watching, look how y2k chic these flipping eyelashes are! So freaking cute, O.M.G!" she exclaims, as she pans both headlights with her camera.

Becky poses with the sunglasses in the front seat and shows her followers her new look. Excited, she shouts to her friend outside the car. "Aw, twin flame, look at how cute I am in these!" she says, then makes duck lips to blow a kiss to her fans. "Hashtag 'living my best life'!" she says, throwing up a peace sign with her fingers. Quickly she motions for her best friend to come closer. "You have to show your fans how cute I am!"

Loving the moment, Chelsea runs to the driver's side to film her. "Such a vibe! So hot!" she says.

Chelsea is done having to entertain the other girl's followers and cuts her off from filming. "Okay, enough," Chelsea states, making a "cut" motion.

Chelsea flips her camera back to face her and addresses her fans. "All right, everyone here's an update; if you're lucky, we might do an impromptu photo shoot with this cute-ass y2k car you just saw.

Let us know your thoughts and tell us what you think in our chat!" Squinching her face, she twists two fingers together. "Fingers crossed you love the idea as much as I do! Eek! Talk to you soon!"

Chelsea and Becky turn their live feeds off in unison.

Becky laughs as she makes eye contact with her friend. "No... Ew. You know we can't do the shoot with this piece of junk. I mean, look, it's a pigsty in here," she says, holding up a bra that was lying on the backseat and pointing to the entire contents of a blue cosmetic bag strewn across the passenger side mat. Noticing a shiny piece of paper on the floor, she leans over and picks it up.

"Yeah, I know, girl, but we have to give something to our followers to up our engagement levels," Chelsea says, rolling her eyes.

Realizing the piece of paper is a torn photo, Becky motions for her friend to be quiet. "Girl, look how cute this is?" she says, holding up the image so she can see young Zoe and her mom. She flips it around to the back, notices a written message, and reads it aloud. "Mommy loves you, Zoe. With love, Brittany."

The heartfelt message makes them both say "ah" and pretend to cry.

Chelsea leans over the passenger side of the car to look at her friend's hand holding the photo. "I can't believe both of you have names that start with the letter B; that's destiny," she says. "When we go inside the festival, we have to find this chick and tell her how cute she and her mom are."

As Becky starts to set the photo back down on the floor she notices a prescription bottle amongst the scattered eyeliner and lipstick. Thinking the design of the plastic looks familiar, she picks it up with excitement. The old amber-colored Xanax container has a partially torn name on the label that reads, "Britt." Becky shakes it to see if anything is inside and laughing at its emptiness she tosses it on the floor. "Definitely should find her; seems like she's our kind of gal," she states.

Chelsea looks in the distance toward the sound stage and becomes impatient. "Let's find a new location to stream from while the lighting is still on point," she says, walking to the back of the car and waiting for her.

Shrugging in agreement, Becky tosses the empty bottle back on the floor and, noticing the radio was on because the car was left running, twists the key in the ignition to turn it off. "She'll def thank me later for that," she says, climbing while out. As she slams the door shut behind her, she flips on the live feed on her social media to document their walk to the official festival grounds.

As the two strut their stuff for their social media feeds and their analytics climb, their matching crochet two-piece outfits flow in the breeze, and the sight of Zoe's vanity plate diminishes in the distance.

About Author

Gitte Tamar

Brigitte, "Gitte," Tamar was born in a small rural Oregon town. Growing up, she was enthralled by scary tales featuring poetic tones and consistently gravitated towards writing darkened narratives. In *Wastoid*, Brigitte explores the harsh realities of social issues faced by today's youth, including the dark outcomes that can be brought on by peer pressure, addiction, homelessness, and abuse. She feels it is essential to share narratives that refrain from sugarcoating the topics society tends to shy away from.